The light at the edge of the sky

Janis Spehr

The light at the edge of the sky

Charlie
through the darkness
never forgotten

The light at the edge of the sky
ISBN 978 1 76109 059 2
Copyright © Janis Spehr 2021
Cover image: sebastian del val from Pixabay

First published 2021 by
GINNINDERRA PRESS
PO Box 3461 Port Adelaide 5015
www.ginninderrapress.com.au

Contents

My goal has been to make my camera a witness of the time in which I live.

The world in my camera – Gisèle Freund

Prologue

The high-ceilinged room is draughty as a cathedral but still warmer than the streets outside.

A man and a girl stand before a painting in the Kaiser Friedrich Museum, Berlin, on an afternoon late in 1920. This outing, a treat for the girl's twelfth birthday next week, is being given by her father who, tall, blond and good-looking, is often mistaken for a northern Protestant. On the anxious edge of puberty, the girl has learned to be vexed that she has not inherited his appearance. Both are well-dressed in the dark, cautious way which befits their class and social standing: these are prosperous, middle-class Jews who have assimilated into a modern, unified nation.

The girl gazes at Jan van Grossaert's *Christ on the Mount of Olives* and tries to pay attention.

'Look hard, Zelli. There's a way of reading a painting and every painting tells a story. This painting is about suffering but also about deception and betrayal.' Her father points out the sleeping disciples. 'There is Peter, who denied Christ three times, and John, the youngest. We are told that he was especially loved by Christ, although,' he says drily, 'this is probably a legacy that has come down to us from the classical Greeks.'

The girl doesn't know what he is talking about. She sees the face of Christ, white and girlish, upturned as he kneels to a white sickle moon surrounded by a shimmering haze. Beneath this halo, a watching angel hovers. She knows that an angel is a messenger from God but she is confused about the rest of the story. 'Who betrayed him?'

Her father indicates Judas in the background, slipping away to the helmeted centurion. 'Always look around the edges, and in the background. That's often where the real story really is. Practise looking. Most people have lazy eyes.'

He tells her about this fifteenth-century Flemish artist, Jan van Grossaert, that he travelled unusually long distances for his time. 'He was one of the first Flemish painters to go to Italy and absorb Italian Renaissance painting. It took three months to reach Italy from Holland.'

The girl imagines deep forests, bandits, wolves, wagons with wooden wheels lurching through mud and storms. Her father has said that, now she is growing up, he will take her regularly to art galleries such as this one, that they will see all the great treasures their country has to offer and that, when she is a little older, he will take her to the Louvre in Paris.

The thought of travel thrills the girl. She sees a train winding through fir trees, crossing the border into France then journeying towards the dense sparkle of light which signals the great city's avenues and boulevards.

She looks again at the figure of the praying Christ begging for deliverance. She looks at the light at the edge of the sky, the dark trees where a person might hide, at the stony crags of the city in deep shadow but she is suddenly bored with this drama and wishes merely for her own deliverance. 'Shall we go for refreshments now, Papa?'

Later, after they leave the café of the Hotel Adlon, where the girl has drunk hot chocolate while her father sipped coffee from a small porcelain cup, they stop on a street corner where a man supports himself with crutches and holds out his cap. The girl's father gives money for which he is thanked but as well as gratitude the girl glimpses something else on the scarred face which is gone before she can name it. It troubles her, makes her vaguely uneasy as she and her father walk towards the tramcar stop. The streets and the big department stores are decorated for Christmas, a festival which her family celebrates (although the tree is always topped with a shining Star of David).

The girl watches everything. There is much that she does not understand but she sees and remembers. There has been a war which her country has lost but now that war is over. She remembers the columns of the casualty lists, how her mother wept for days when first Uncle Theo, then Uncle Willi was killed. Then, the newspapers had been full of words like 'patriotism', 'glory', 'sacrifice'. Now she sees different words: 'betrayal'; 'dishonour'.

Snow begins to fall. Amid the swarms of shoppers on the street, the girl makes out a man with an eyepatch and one arm wearing a sign around his neck. She strains to see its lettering but the tram clatters on. She turns up the black velvet collar of her coat then snuggles her hands again in the grey squirrel muff bought recently at Weitheims. When she and her father reach their destination, there will be the warmth of the big apartment and her mother bustling about, giving orders to Maria and Teresa as they prepare the evening meal. There will be candlelight through glass, a family eating soup, fish and meat with silver cutlery and drinking wine from crystal.

The girl turns to her father. 'These men, the ones who are everywhere…'

Her father smiles. He is not normally demonstrative, either with herself or her brother, but now he takes one of her hands from the muff and squeezes it gently. He says, 'Germany will rise again.'

Part One

Paris

High shiny black boots

21 December 1941

> Whenever you heard boots at night you let them alone. Boots were German.
> *Sylvia Beach and the lost generation: a history of literary Paris in the twenties and thirties* – Noel Riley Fitch

Sylvia wakes from a half-remembered dream, something to do with a dark animal, crouched outside a shuttered place, pinioning her with its stare. This image stays with her, vaguely disturbing, like the shadow of a raised hand, while she watches the small window lighten from black to bluish-grey. When she hears the first soft stutter from the pigeons she lights the rose-coloured oil lamp next to the bed. The lamp was an anniversary gift from Adrienne, years ago; Sylvia wishes she could remain near its small halo of light for the rest of the day. It's so cold that she knows that she will have to break the coating of ice in the jug which contains the water for her morning wash. She lies beneath the quilt, trying to recall the rest of the dream. She's not usually introspective – she leaves that to the artists and writers whose work lines the walls and shelves of her shop – but, for reasons she can't explain, illuminating these fragments from her unconscious seems important.

It's no use procrastinating. Reluctantly, Sylvia leaves her cocoon, reaches beneath her bed for the ceramic pot, the rim of which is patterned with roses and violets, then carries it down the stairs, where she empties its murky contents into the toilet on the landing. Shivering, she re-enters the apartment then stands at the dresser in her bedroom, bathing her face and hands in the large basin. The other room of the apartment holds a desk and her books as well as a table and two chairs for the rare occasions she sits down to do something other than write. She has lived here for more than four years, since she came back from the United States to find another woman in Adrienne's bed. Momentarily, Sylvia closes her eyes as though by so doing she will leave the crust on that wound intact.

When she opens them the mirror hanging from a nail above the basin gives back a still, seamed mask. Its sharp features are not yet wizened but that will come soon. As she faces her reflection, Sylvia realises that she won't be able to keep lying about her age for much longer; even going through Customs on that ill-fated journey back to France in 1937, the clerk, after checking her passport, had regarded her quizzically. Her mother always taught that vanity was a curse (how clever Cyprian had become at smuggling make-up home when she and Sylvia were girls!); a sexual snare that made women ultimately unhappy. Yet she wanted us to look attractive, Sylvia thinks, like nice girls, like ladies, a credit to her training, and Daddy's as well. She searches in the mirror for her young face: strong, almost valorous in its determination, the mouth compressed but the eyes glowing and defiant. Part of her can't understand why it's not still there.

She pulls on her skirt, knots the foulard tie of her blue shirt into its customary floppy bow. She passes through her study, with its unlit stove and bare walls, contemplating breakfast. She's half-inclined to skip it and go straight to Shakespeare & Company but she knows if she doesn't eat now, she will crash mid-morning and this is one of the things which can bring on the ringing pain in her head that lays her low for days. She shrugs into the navy wool coat which is her greatest friend on these mornings. It's looser: during the last few months, she has been losing weight steadily. The strain of the war, the effects of grief, the daily battle to survive have all hollowed her out. And not just physically: as Sylvia descends the stairs, she thinks about the ongoing struggle to keep her business afloat. For years now her shop – famous, beloved, the haunt of the most influential writers of the time – has been a sinking ship on a sea of trouble. If it hadn't been for the help of sympathetic friends, particularly Bryher, whose father had actually owned a shipping line, well...

The cold makes her gasp as she starts along the rue de l'Odéon, pausing three doors down, but she won't take the chance of waking Adrienne, even though she usually rises early.

Sylvia quickens her pace. The curfew is over; on the foggy street, people pass each other like phantoms. If she keeps moving, the cold and hunger won't win and the people who have caused them won't win either. She turns into rue Rotrou hoping that she will be able to travel the short distance to the Café Voltaire unimpeded. For reasons only known to themselves, the Germans continually block off thoroughfares so that pedestrians (and most of the population are pedestrians now) are forced to backtrack and re-route. Civilians can never predict where and when this might happen. A person might turn confidently into a well-known avenue, only to find her progress halted by a barricade of sandbags; she might plan a foraging expedition for the steadily diminishing amount of foodstuffs on offer then have to redraw the map she carries in her head. Paris has become an ever-changing labyrinth; this familiar place, her home for years, is now disorienting and strange.

But this morning, nothing prevents a direct journey. She sits at a table in the café and hurriedly consumes thin coffee and a grey flabby thing imitating a croissant. The pastry flakes on her plate look like dandruff from someone elderly and sick. Nearby conversations are muted, the aural equivalent of the dim light outside. Nobody speaks loudly any more; who knows what stories someone might carry to those who daily control the lives of all citizens? An atmosphere of distrust and disenchantment is palpable, thicker and more oppressive than the frigid air outside.

Sylvia retraces her steps, pulling her coat around her tightly as the wind sweeps down. The fog has given way to drizzle. She passes the orthopaedic shoemaker then the music shop with its display of varnished violins. As she reaches Shakespeare & Company, she slips and stumbles on the rain-slicked street. This happened once before, years ago, as she walked with James Joyce. She would have fallen had he not clutched her arm and righted her. *Cher madame*, take care, he had said, in the soft brogue which decades of living in Europe never diminished.

How courteous Joyce had been, how charming, Sylvia thinks, as she unlocks the shop. But utterly selfish and disregarding of everyone's welfare where his writing was concerned. His constant financial demands and his financial betrayal, cutting her out of money from the American publication of *Ulysses* in 1936, had bankrupted her business; would have bankrupted her health, too, if it hadn't been for Adrienne's intervention. When Joyce had told her he didn't want her to have the money, Sylvia had been sick for a week.

As the door opens, his face looks back at her. The photographs Berenice Abbott made in 1926 show him well-dressed and retiring, reluctant to face the camera. He wears an eyepatch which gives him a faintly sinister air but also emphasises his frailty. In the photographs from the 1928 sitting, he is more confident and relaxed, with a hat tilted at an almost rakish angle, but his gaze is melancholy and self-absorbed, fixed on some twilight point in the middle distance.

When, at the beginning of the year, Sylvia had learned that a stomach ulcer had killed Joyce, she felt the same mix of emotions which her father's death a few months previously had provoked: loss and relief. For Sylvester; thankfulness that he was no longer reduced to drooling incontinence; for Joyce, on whose behalf she had struggled for so long, knowledge that he had lived long enough to do everything that was in him to do. Joyce had reached the end of his particular journey with language and language was what he lived for: what would have been the point of him continuing?

Sylvia gazes across the street to Adrienne's shop, remembering the times she spent there with Joyce then she goes to the table where she keeps her accounts and examines the foolscap-sized book with the borrowing records for her lending library. This number, which has been declining steadily since the beginning of the war, is now very small. Simone de Beauvoir, schoolteacher and friend of Jean-Paul Sartre, has been in recently, along with a few others. That's all. On the table there is also a package of books for Paul Valéry, done up in brown paper and string. He won't come into the shop now because some of the Germans do. She must remember to post it.

Sylvia looks at the clock on the wall which shows one minute to nine. She turns the 'Closed' sign on the door round. She dusts then sweeps. These mundane activities soothe her. She is crouched down, re-arranging some books on a low shelf when she hears the click, click, click along the pavement.

The sound is crisp, spaced at regular intervals. Now that there are hardly any cars left in Paris, she is used to the sound of footsteps but these have a particular rhythm and a tone which is different from the clopping of wooden soles or the swift scuffle of rubber. She sees the boots as the door opens, through a space made by a table.

There's a moment of silence as the boots pause; then they walk, in no particular hurry, across the shop floor. They gleam with an almost metallic sheen; or perhaps their lustre more closely resembles the gloss on the coat of a highly trained, well-bred animal.

Sylvia rises and straightens. The man has his back to her; his shoulders are straight, his attention seemingly given to the volume he is perusing. The uniform is the one she expected. Her visitor is fairly tall, with the broad-shouldered, slim-hipped physique considered pleasing in men. Dark reddish-brown hair slopes neatly from beneath his cap. He puts the book back on the shelf. His eyes skim the Berenice Abbot photos: there's Janet Flanner, wearing striped trousers and a top hat, crop-haired Jane Heap dressed in a tuxedo and beautiful Margaret Anderson draped with a fox fur.

Sylvia tenses. For an insane moment, she thinks the man will spit but he just continues his inspection.

She moves across her shop and positions herself slightly behind him and to his left. 'Can I help you with something, sir?'

In these situations, she always attempts to create a demilitarised zone, with carefully chosen remarks about Goethe's poetry and Schiller's dramatic tragedies (although she is equally careful not to mention Heine.)

He turns and smiles. He doesn't answer her but Sylvia can't tell whether this is due to lack of courtesy or lack of English. Instead, he steps away from her to examine another group of photographs quarantined in the lower right-hand corner on the wall.

This collection is much more recent and dates from the last years of the thirties: there are photographs of André Breton, Jean-Paul Sartre, Virginia Woolf and James Joyce. These are portraits taken by Gisèle Freund. Sylvia's never liked them and only displays them out of loyalty to Adrienne. This is not because they were taken by the woman who turned her out of Adrienne's bed; no, not at all: Sylvia has always found them aesthetically displeasing. They are colour photographs but not the painstaking, hand-tinted colour done by underpaid women with sable brushes a few hairs fine. These are composed of layers of chemical dye which are shifty and unstable: if exposed to too much direct sunlight, they sometimes give back shades which are unrealistic to the point of surreal. This has started to happen to several of the photos displayed. Certain skin tones are sliding towards magenta; yellows have taken on the hue of decayed teeth; greens are shaded like bathroom mould.

Sylvia's suggestion to Gisèle, that she photograph Joyce in colour, was partly malicious. Sylvia didn't think Joyce would consent. However, she has to admit that the photo which appeared on the cover of *Time* magazine in 1939 almost does him justice. The rust-red velvet jacket he wears is a perfect foil for his face, pale, aged and worn with illness, as he bends over a page with a large magnifying glass. It is an image at once thoroughly modern yet reminiscent of a fifteenth-century Flemish oil painting with its paradox of opulent asceticism.

The man in uniform gazes at it thoughtfully. Sylvia wants him out of Shakespeare & Company. In twenty minutes, François will be here. The man in uniform must not meet François. If he wants the photo of Joyce, Sylvia will sell it, just to be rid of him. She reaches her decision just as the man turns to her again.

'This artist,' he says casually, in perfect English, 'I knew her years ago, in Berlin.'

His remark takes Sylvia by surprise: what on earth would Gisèle have in common with this soldier? But then, if Gisèle had known him when she was young, Germany would have been a very different place to the one it now is.

Sylvia strives for a neutral tone, utters the first banality that springs to mind. 'Miss Freund's a very talented lady.'

Her visitor laughs softly. 'Oh, yes, she's clever.'

As he resumes his patrol of Shakespeare & Company, Sylvia gets a queasy feeling, as though Jean-Paul Sartre, so grave and decorous in the photograph on the wall, has suddenly turned and presented his other profile, the one with the cast eye. The officer runs his hand lingeringly down the spine of Valéry's *La Soiree avec Monsieur Teste*. The eyes beneath his grey and black cap with its silver insignia are brown, flecked with green, and intelligent. He wears a wedding ring. He moves as though he has been coming here for years and this attitude, which is so relaxed, completely at home, makes her fists curl; but suddenly everything, including prepared remarks about German poetry, is driven from her mind when the man abruptly stops his perusal.

'I understand you hold a copy of *Finnegan's Wake*.'

He knows perfectly well Sylvia has the book. It's displayed in her shop window like a holy relic, open at the page where 'Shaun the fiery boy shouted, naturally incensed, as he shook the red pepper out of his auricles…' It's a proofing copy given to Sylvia by Joyce just before the book was published in 1939 and it's also signed by him.

Sylvia calls on all her reserves of charm, all her years of cajoling and soothing prickly temperaments and arrogant egos, as she smiles and replies. 'I'm sorry, sir. That book's not for sale.'

Her visitor doesn't seem to hear. 'I'm very interested in modern writers, particularly Joyce. I have a degree in literature and spent some time before the war at Cambridge University.'

I don't care whether you hold a PhD in astrophysics from the Sorbonne, thinks Sylvia. Here is a member of the army which has overrun half of Europe, caused the death and departure of dear friends and turned the city she loves into a place of fear and privation: he will not have her book.

'It's not for sale.'

Why won't somebody enter the shop? Not even in the financially distressed Depression years has Sylvia wished so fervently for customers. One of the very few American expatriates who still remain in Paris after all the disasters of the thirties; some students seeking English or American novels: any of these would do (but not Françoise or Ruth, the two young women who occasionally assist her.) Then, for the first time, Sylvia sees the car, dark and sleek, parked a little further down the street and answers her own question.

A pulse jumps at the German's throat and his mildly ruddy complexion is a shade darker but he says nothing, just walks to the other side of the shop. Sylvia watches him the way she would watch a tiger with its cage door open. She expects him to fling a photograph onto the floor and have the glass carapace shatter to shards; or perhaps he will consign a shelf of books to the floor with a single sweep of one elegantly clad arm. But he does nothing so vulgar.

He looks at his watch then glances outside. 'I will come back,' he says pleasantly then leaves the shop, quietly closing the door.

Sylvia hears the sound of his boots as they click across the pavement. A flunkey, wearing a uniform of inferior cut and fabric to his master's, holds open the car door.

As soon as the car is out of sight, Sylvia takes the book from the window and stashes it in the nearest cupboard. (She remembers, inconsequentially, that Ernest Hemingway always refers to it jokily as *Finnigan's Wank*, even though he admires the book and its author.) Then she slumps to the floor. Briefly she imagines remaining here forever, head resting against her arms crossed on her bent knees but when she opens her eyes and looks up, her glance encounters Germaine Krull's streetscape of the stone lion in the Place de la Concorde, with the obelisk and the Eiffel Tower in the background. This photograph, perhaps more than any other, has always symbolised the beauty and history of her adopted city, the city now servile and plundered.

Sylvia forces herself up. She hurries to the door. Her hands shake; she drops the key on the ground, and has to make two attempts to fit it in the lock. When the shop is finally secure, she crosses the rue d'Odéon, knowing that by now Adrienne will be in her shop. As she approaches *La maison des amis des livres*, there's a telltale silver ripple at the edge of her vision, followed by a sudden darkening, as though clouds have crossed a malignant sun

When she pushes open the door, she sees Adrienne with several students from the Sorbonne who are earnestly soliciting her opinion about Surrealist poetry.

'Any work of art that can be understood is the work of a journalist,' Adrienne tells them.

In spite of everything, Sylvia smiles. It is typical of Adrienne's generosity that she will quote the words of André Breton, a man she has never liked. He had been in the shop, a handsome blustery youth wearing a French army uniform, the very first day she met Adrienne, in 1917. Adrienne had got rid of him, but less gently and persuasively than the way she now deflects the group of students, who seem prepared to stay for the remainder of the morning.

When they finally leave, Sylvia pours out the story of her imperilled treasure. 'A German officer…' The silver ripples in her head widen and begin their blade-like work.

Adrienne listens gravely. Her fine high forehead, still barely lined, crinkles slightly. The gaze from her hazel eyes is luminous, serious, tender, the gaze she usually turns on the world. As usual, she is dressed in a floor-length grey skirt, and wears an embroidered blue vest over a white blouse beneath a short grey cape. Despite rationing, she has not lost weight, a fact Sylvia finds disconcerting and wonderful.

'Times have changed,' Adrienne says when Sylvia pauses. 'Now that your country is at war, you must expect things to be different. You're no longer protected by those big red seals.' She is referring to the official markings made by someone from the United States embassy which mark Shakespeare & Company as a business owned by an American national; but since they were placed there, the Japanese have bombed Pearl Harbour.

'Come here,' Adrienne orders, gently.

Sylvia puts her head down against the soft pillows of Adrienne's breasts and closes her eyes. This is her only remaining sanctuary, the reason that, despite the urging of family and friends, she chose to remain in France. Their relationship has come full circle: first there was friendship, followed by passion; then a rupture, soon repaired. Now their friendship, never discussed, is something as necessary as water or air to them both

'I've hidden the book. What will I do if he returns?'

Adrienne is silent. For once, Sylvia realises, she has no solution.

'There is nothing more you can do. Try to put it out of your mind. He may forget about it.' One of her hands hovers above Sylvia's left temple but does not touch it; this touch might make Sylvia cry out.

Adrienne has tried over the years to mitigate these ferocious outbursts of pain but the cause of the migraines is impossible to eradicate. Adrienne is as powerless against the legacy of Sylvia's Calvinist guilt and repression as she is against the predatory soldier. She only knows that Odéonia, the name she gives to the two bookshops, the country without passports or armies which she and Sylvia have created, is now threatened.

She holds Sylvia tighter. 'Stay with me.'

'No, I must go.'

Sylvia leaves *La maison des amis des livres* weaving like a drunk. She can't see. Her matt-black world is filled with pulsing silver striations. She crosses the street and stumbles up the stairs to her apartment, glad that she has at least been spared the indignity of being sick in public. Memories of her father outside the door of her mother's bedroom late at night, 'Please let me come in. I'm your husband,' and her mother's reply, the growl of a frightened animal, flood her mind.

There's the squat metal bucket she left beneath the tap this morning, waiting to be filled with cold water. Sylvia makes it just in time. The vomit splatters in stars.

Potassons

Tuesday, 23 December 1941

Adrienne decapitates the chicken, plucks it then wrenches out the guts. For reasons over which she has no control, it arrived from her parents' village a few days earlier than anticipated. The man who delivered it this morning was bound on a mission to who knows where from Rocfoin and clearly regarded the chicken as a flapping nuisance when he handed it over to her in its wooden crate, together with a parcel of plump tomatoes. Adrienne had considered keeping the chicken alive for a few days but where would she get feed for it and then there was the mess it would make, so, this year, *Le reveillon de Noël* has had to be sacrificed on the altar of practicality. She has wrung the chicken's neck briskly and it now lies, minus head and feet, next to a pile of russet-gold feathers.

Adrienne has telephoned her sister and Paul Valéry. She has saved bread to make a stuffing and plucked rosemary and oregano, grown in a window box. Nearly everyone in Paris is a gardener now, turning the soil in parkland and raising rabbits in backyards, anything to supplement the inadequate rations. Only those prepared to bed down with the conquerors (and this doesn't just extend to the hard-working brothel employees) can be assured of a full stomach. Adrienne knows that Sylvia never intended that Ernest Hemingway's remark would find its way back to its original target: 'Adrienne's always thinking of her belly. Let's hope she doesn't crawl on it to the Krauts, in order to have food to fill it.'

Adrienne reflects that Hemingway is a gifted writer but has the emotional maturity of a six-year-old. The blonde American journalist he married recently seems a match; nevertheless, Adrienne doubts their union will last. She knows Hem: his mother dressed him as a girl until he was seven years old and, ever since, he has constantly surpassed himself in efforts to show that he is not.

Adrienne burrows into her small hoard of potatoes and turnips, rinses those she selects and takes up a peeling knife. She wishes for greens, something verdant and crisp to counteract all that starch; even a bunch of wild nettles, picked from the side of a country road, would do. She looks through the window out to the street which wears a film of grey ice. It is late afternoon and almost dark. Even this room, painted violet with rough red linen curtains at the windows (thank you, Gisèle), doesn't lend warmth to the freezing air. The oven, with just enough coal to cook this feast, will provide a little heat.

If hunger has a colour, then it is whiteness, Adrienne thinks, sitting down suddenly, a faint trilling in her ears. White is what she sees when she's hungry. She breathes deeply through her nose, in, then out, and the room returns with its striped Turkish rug and her brother-in-law's framed charcoal sketches on the walls. Adrienne takes up the red suns of her father's tomatoes and places them in a gold-edged dish patterned with green and crimson poppies. Later on, she'll prepare them in a casserole with onions but now all she wants to do is look at them; they're a reminder of times when food preparation was something satisfying, an act of conviviality and generosity, rather than a struggle born of bleak necessity. Also, the tomatoes bring back memories of her father in his garden, swearing amiably at his wife because she wanted to replace some of his painstakingly tended vegetables with several lines of snapdragons and alliums.

This morning's stranger had assured her that Clovis and Philiberte were both well. Adrienne wants more than anything to confirm it for herself but there is no petrol for the Citroën in which Sylvia used to chauffeur her before the war.

Adrienne shakes her head slightly. Brooding is pointless. She must keep moving around; it is the only way she will keep warm. When she turns round to put the dish on the table, Walter Benjamin is sitting there, smiling.

'Well,' Adrienne says, 'you took your time.' She believes that human beings are more spirit than matter and that the spiritual element continues after death. She has been expecting this visit, eventually.

Benjamin makes no reply. He wears a rumpled white shirt under a dark green cardigan and looks very much as he did when Adrienne last saw him sitting at this table with herself, Sylvia and Bryher towards the end of 1939.

'Please, stay a while,' Adrienne says, in her best hostess mode.

When she learned of Benjamin's suicide on the Spanish border last year as he fled from the encroaching Germans, she had mourned the loss of that brilliant subtle mind, the books which would never now be written. However, she's pleased he is with her now. She will not tell Sylvia. Her greatest friend is sceptical about the afterlife in a typical Anglo-Saxon, post-Protestant way, although always happy to lay out the tarot.

Anyway, Sylvia was never as close to Walter as Adrienne had been, all their hours spent in discussion as they delved into philosophy and mysticism, searching, seeking…

Adrienne takes a tomato and slices it, still watched by the smiling apparition. 'Well, you always did like my cooking.'

At the dinner in 1939, there had been another roast chicken, as well as trout then meringues for desert. Less wine than usual had been consumed because Bryher is a teetotaller. (Here Adrienne, preparing her Christmas feast, casts her eyes to the ceiling. She loves England and its people but sometimes they're hard to understand. She can't imagine life without wine.)

This was before the conquerors had come sweeping in a grey shroud through the Arc de Triomphe, when it was not thought possible that there would be a repeat of 1870, France a defeated nation with, this time around, no hope of buying its freedom. Bryher had already begun using her father's money to aid people escaping Germany, channelling them through Switzerland and away to England and America. Adrienne thinks back to the events leading up to that time: the fall of the Popular Front, the election of Daladier's xenophobic government, the quarantining of suspect refugees. Arthur Koestler had turned up one night, dirty and scared, on the run after escaping from the camp where he had been interned for four months. When he had gone, several anxious days later, she and Sylvia had had to fumigate the apartment because Arthur left lice as a parting gift.

Then there were other exiles: André Breton has fled, taking his wife and child to the United States.

'Trust him to survive,' Adrienne says to Walter Benjamin as she slices onions briskly, letting tears sit unchecked on her cheeks. Despite all Breton's proclamations of brotherly *esprit* and solidarity with the working masses, he'd always look after number one. 'Indeed,' she continues, 'what were all those surrealist manifestoes about except ego, ego, ego, beating people verbally into submission until they toed his party line, whatever that happened to be at that particular time?' Wealthy patrons protect Breton from care in the New World. Adrienne hopes he stays there. She has no concern for him; unlike Gisèle, who is never far from her thoughts.

'Can you help me with that?' she asks but when she looks up from the table, her old friend has vanished. No matter: he'll return. Adrienne sautés the onions, with her mind still on Walter's fellow *émigré*.

Gisèle. Gisèle had been a burst of electricity after years of gentle gaslight. Not that 'gentle' was a descriptor that you would readily apply to Sylvia (although she was, of course, in the best sense.)

Adrienne turns the chicken, bastes it, slides the casserole into the oven, then straightens, grunting softly as she eases the strain in her lower back.

By the time Adrienne encountered Gisèle that afternoon in 1934, she and Sylvia had shared a life together for fifteen years. Their original passion had blurred, through habit and familiarity, into a midlife relationship which was steady, strong and predictable. Gisèle had been in her twenties, vivid and mercurial, mesmerised by light. Forged in the conflagrations of the Weimar Republic, her idealism tempered by Marxist social theory studied under Theodor Adorno, she challenged Adrienne; sometimes shocked her.

Adrienne recalls one afternoon in 1936: Gisèle, somewhat sweaty and dishevelled after roaming the streets for hours with her Leica, entering *La maison des amis des livres* to find Jacques Benoist-Mechin browsing.

'What's he doing here?' she had hissed.

Adrienne, taken aback by this breach of *politesse*, had spoken reprovingly. 'Monsieur Benoist-Mechin helped me with the translation of *Ulysses* into French. He's a charming, cultivated man.'

'He's a charming, cultivated Fascist!'

Benoist-Mechin's recent membership of the ultra right-wing French People's Party had surprised no one.

'Please lower your voice, Gisèle,' because people had turned to stare at their exchange.

'I'll lower my voice when he leaves the shop!'

'That's for me to say, who comes into my shop, or doesn't.'

Benoist-Mechin, not at all put out, had approached, smiling. Gisèle had pointedly turned her back then exited shortly afterwards, not saying another word.

'Please forgive my friend,' Adrienne had said.

'Ah, well, those people, they're so often abrasive, aren't they?' Benoist-Mechin had replied, still smiling.

For the first time, Adrienne had caught a whiff of something oozing from beneath the urbane exterior. 'And which people would they be, monsieur?' she had asked softly, but her only answer was an opaque smile.

There is a clatter of footsteps on the stairs and a smell of burning pine, a scent Adrienne always associates with energy and American enthusiasm, qualities which are the essence of Sylvia, who rushes into the apartment, a covered plate in one hand and a cloth-wrapped item in the other. They embrace, Adrienne thinking once again that if Sylvia becomes any thinner she will vanish. What little flesh she had has disappeared; now, her vitality is concentrated solely in her bones. She feels brittle as a summer twig.

'So,' she says, kissing Adrienne briskly then lighting a cigarette, 'who are we expecting this evening?'

'Just Rinette, Émile-Paul and Fargue – and I've asked Valéry as well.'

'Ah!' says Sylvia. 'A gathering of *potassons*.'

This is Fargue's word that he created and used playfully about the group of closest friends who had clustered around Adrienne's shop in its early years, people distinguished by their kindness and *joie de vivre*. Its use always evokes the beginning of the friendship between Sylvia and herself and the struggles and successes they have shared.

She hugs her comrade in letters once more then disengages herself and peers at Sylvia's bundles. 'What treasures have you here?'

Sylvia discards the piece of pale blue cloth.

'Oh,' says Adrienne, 'a piece of ice. 'How thoughtful of you, sweetheart.'

Inside the shard of ice is an embalmed flower, a tousled yellow head above a green stalk.

'Daisy, daisy, give me your answer, do,' sings Sylvia, half a tone flat and making Adrienne place her hands over her ears. 'I'm half crazy, all for the love of you,' and she launches into a story from her New England girlhood involving her older sister in a dress with leg-o-mutton sleeves and a beau wearing a straw boater.

The flower is not a daisy, just a dandelion, but as Adrienne holds its gleaming carapace, dripping, to the window she reflects that in this moribund city it's a miracle that Sylvia has found even this humble weed preserved. She places the knife of ice in the sink.

'We could eat it,' she suggests, 'or use it as a garnish.'

This makes them both laugh.

Sylvia takes Adrienne's arm and swings her around. 'But you'll look sweet, upon a seat of a bicycle built for two,' she warbles.

They move around the kitchen with practised ease, laying out cutlery and glasses and choosing wine from Adrienne's now very limited stock. The bottles selected do not include the Moet & Chandon Brut Imperial 1914. She keeps this for the day when the occupiers are finally driven from the city.

For dessert, Sylvia has bought six small cakes from the Café Voltaire. Adrienne doesn't ask how she came by them. Sylvia, incurably gregarious, has the ability to strike up friendships with all kinds of people. Clearly, she's on good terms with someone there. The cakes look anaemic because they contain whitish lard, not butter; in contrast, they are plastered with bloody icing garishly infused with cochineal. They will taste like nothing but are better than nothing. To Adrienne, a meal without dessert is almost desecration. Pre-war, her pastry-making marathons were legendary, her golden crumbling flan bases crowned with glazed berries and apricots. This year, there's not even chocolate for the *buche de Noël*, the festive Christmas roll.

Thoughts of chocolate make Adrienne think of Henri Michaux, who is addicted to chocolate in the way some people are addicted to morphine or cocaine and who has always maintained that he cannot work without it.

'It's a good thing Henri is in the Free Zone,' she says to Sylvia.

'I doubt that it's readily available there, either.'

Everyone has heard the stories which belie the confident propaganda which comes out of Marshall Petain's Vichy France. Shortages of most foods must make Henri wish he was back in pre-war Latin America, watching cocoa beans being harvested.

'Imagine,' Sylvia muses, drying her hands on a tea towel, 'the Aztecs drank chocolate while they watched someone's heart being torn out and held up to the sun. Henri would adore the surreal violence of that image.'

'Henri would adore the idea of the image, perhaps not the image itself.' They discuss the gifted, enigmatic Belgian's idiosyncratic literature and art until, just as Adrienne takes her grandmother's dinner service from the cupboard beneath the sink, they're plunged into darkness.

'Oh, fuck!' Sylvia exclaims, although they should be used to power cuts by now.

She and Adrienne get out candles (made from the same white lard which goes into the pastry) and place them strategically around the small dining room. When this is done, it's transformed into a cave of flickering light, a subtle place of shadow and glow. As Adrienne pours out two glasses of wine, she sees that the ice encasing the dandelion has melted and, when Sylvia's not looking, she throws the wilting weed into the garbage before they both draw their chairs nearer to the warmth.

'Look at this filth.' Sylvia produces a three-day-old copy of the openly collaborationist paper *Je suis partout,* and points to one of its cartoons. France is shown as a helpless maiden attempting to struggle free from the assorted clutches of Communists, Jews and Freemasons. Clustered coyly nearby, surrounding a baby designated as 'Europe' are a number of other maidens: Holland, Belgium, Denmark, Croatia, all the countries the Germans have conquered. 'Don't wait any longer if you want to part of this family' runs the inscription underneath.

'Really shows the inherent misogyny of Nazi ideology,' Sylvia observes caustically. 'We're just poor weak creatures in need of protection, fit only to be used as breeding stock.'

Adrienne smiles appreciatively as she shovels the last of the coal into the fire. The cartoon is just one example of the propaganda they are forced to endure every day. They both loathe Robert Brasillach, the paper's pig-eyed editor, a long-time Fascist committed to collaboration.

Adrienne, who has a strong belief in karma, says, gazing into the flames, 'His time will come.'

This conversation depresses them, so they are both pleased when Paul Valéry arrives. Adrienne left the invitation open, thinking there would be enough food to go around if his current mistress or his son, François, chose to accompany him, but the gentle, stooping septuagenarian with the tobacco-stained moustache has come alone. (Madame Valéry and her daughter never accompany him on these evenings; they remain cloistered in their spacious home like the decent, middle-class Frenchwomen they are.)

Valéry carries a book and embraces them in turn. 'Ah, Sylvia,' he says, holding her at arm's length while she smiles back.

For once. words fail them: the dense web of puns, witticism and allusions which constitute their dialogue cannot describe their current situation. He glances distastefully at the cartoon Adrienne and Sylvia have been discussing.

Rinette and Émile-Paul arrive soon after. Émile-Paul pours more wine. No one knows where Léon-Paul Fargue is but no one expresses concern. Fargue's lateness is legendary, the bane of every hostess who is not prepared to accommodate his idiosyncratic night-wandering ways. He has been known to arrive two weeks late for a dinner party. He will show up when he is ready, or, perhaps, not at all.

Adrienne takes the duvet off her bed for Sylvia; there are just enough rugs and shawls to go around. They all huddle at the table while the chicken is carved. Everyone exclaims about its size, the tenderness of the flesh beneath the basted, golden skin. All the potatoes, turnips and casserole disappear. Nobody seems to miss green vegetables.

They start in on Sylvia's tough little pastries.

When Valéry learns of the effort expended to procure them, he remarks, 'Sylvia, I'm glad your charm and ingenuity has not desserted you.'

Everyone groans; Valéry smiles in a self-deprecating manner. Adrienne spoons bitter chicory syrup into cups to make the thin brew they despise. They curse the Germans for taking away their right to drink decent coffee. Despite this, the drink warms them as does the gossip which has always been their lifeblood. Émile-Paul mentions that he saw Simone de Beauvoir yesterday at the Café de Flore.

'No Germans there,' murmurs Valéry, who himself would never set foot in the Flore, with its clientele of semi-employed actresses, kept women and aspiring directors.

'But you should have seen her! Skin like an angel's, as though lit from the inside, translucent as Garbo's.' Emile-Paul is in raptures.

'Yes, malnutrition can be so glamorous,' Sylvia comments drily.

'Well, it doesn't seem to be having that effect on any of us,' says Adrienne. She glances affectionately at her brother-in-law, artist and pornographer, then at Rinette, her little sister, so unlike Adrienne, with her high cheekbones and dark hair. 'You said you were bringing something to show us.'

The cloth which Rinette unfolds from her bag is a piece of embroidery which shows a waterbird standing in a pool beneath a full moon, executed in silk thread, black, silver, very dark green and midnight blue. Hours of painstaking work have gone into making it. Adrienne reflects that if men produced such things, they would be regarded as high art and have the same status as Valéry's poems; as it is, tapestry is usually designated as merely decorative, unless it has some historical significance.

Not that Valéry is at all dismissive. He examines the embroidery closely. 'So beautiful, Marie.' (He never uses her nickname.) 'Exquisite. I can only offer words.'

'You have some for us, then?' Adrienne asks rhetorically.

Valéry opens the book he has brought and reads, 'The graveyard by the sea', written in 1917; one of those poems which broke his twenty-year literary silence.

Adrienne draws her cape more closely around her and sits listening to the rise and swell of the language. Nineteen-seventeen, that year of horror and catastrophe, was the time Valéry first came into *La maison des amis des livres*.

When he reaches the final stanza, his frail voice crests:

> The wind is rising!… We must try to live!
> The huge air opens and shuts my book: the wave
> Dares to explode out of the rocks in reeking
> Spray. Fly away, my sun-bewildered pages!

Through half-closed eyes, Adrienne sees Sylvia throw her head back, in the same way she once did as she approached orgasm.

> Break, waves! Break up with your rejoicing surges
> This quiet roof where sails like doves were pecking.

There is silence for a few moments. Valéry closes the book. The fire has gone out and the effort of reading has brought a bluish tinge to his lips. He lights a cigarette and inhales. The smoke hangs in the air, a pale veil dissipating the trance cast by his words.

Rinette is the first to speak. 'What news of Veronique?'

Adrienne says quietly, 'There's been no news for some time.'

It had been Fargue's idea, the code name which invokes the patron saint of photography, the woman who wiped Christ's face with a square of linen on his way to the Cross.

'No one knows exactly where she is. It's possible she moves around, in order to be safe. She took her camera but I can't think she's working in Vichy…'

'Her camera? She took her camera? Surely there are penalties for an alien having one of those?' Émile-Paul interjects.

Adrienne shrugs. 'You know Veronique. She once told me that without a camera, she feels like an amputee. When she left Germany in '33, she smuggled out some of her most important negatives, even though she knew the penalties would be severe if she were caught.'

Valéry says, musingly, 'I understand some people are having quite a reasonable life in the Free Zone…

'Not if they are people like Veronique,' Adrienne retorts.

She loves Valéry, reveres his poetry but his overwhelming regard for the intellect at the expense of all else sometimes exasperates her: it isolates him from ordinary life. Valéry still cherishes some respect for General Pétain, the octogenarian ruler of southern France, the part that the Germans have graciously left 'free'. But Adrienne doesn't trust the World War One hero any more than the members of the poisonous coterie which surrounds him. She thinks Pierre Laval is evil, just waiting for a word from the Germans to unleash a reign of terror against the Jews who have taken refuge in Vichy.

However, because she loves him, she looks mildly at Valéry and changes the subject. 'I've always thought her portrait of you was one of the best in the exhibition.'

She is referring to the 1939 show of Gisèle's work where portraits of some of the best known artists and writers of their generation were projected onto a screen in *La maison des amis des livres:* as well as Valéry and Adrienne, there was Michaux, Joyce, Breton and the English novelist Virginia Woolf. 'You are a poet of the face,' Adrienne had said, taking Gisèle's hands in her own.

Now, Valéry demurs with Adrienne's assessment; he believes André Malraux's portrait was the most psychologically acute, catches some dissembling quality which is the essence of that political charmer.

They are all recalling their particular favourites, the afternoon on the eve of the war when the subjects gathered to view their facsimiles, when Sylvia interrupts.

'You know, it's a very strange thing, the officer in my shop the other day wanting Mr Joyce's book was asking after Gis… Veronique, said that he had known her in Germany before the war.' She throws this rather lightly into the conversation, as a curio, and is completely unprepared for the tremor which crosses Adrienne's face. Sylvia reads shock, dismay then an anger which is quickly suppressed.

'Perhaps not so strange.' Émile-Paul hasn't noticed and just sips his chicory. 'He may have attended university in Frankfurt with her. May have even been a friend of hers, once.'

Everyone is silent again, remembering the seismic shifts in alliances which characterised the twenties and thirties in the riven Weimar Republic. There, the ideological ground was always unstable, combustible.

Valéry lifts his glass. 'Well, a toast to Veronique, wherever she is.'

Adrienne opens her mouth to include 'absent friends' then shuts it again. Some wounds are still too raw and she can't mention those who are gone forever, like Walter, like Virginia Woolf who earlier in the year walked into a river with her pockets weighted with stone. So much has been lost, so much destroyed. Tears cloud her eyes. Sylvia takes her hand.

They drink the toast then talk of other things until the looming curfew forces Valéry to his feet.

'Well, how glad I am to be part of *this* family,' he remarks, as he winds a woollen scarf around his neck.

They laugh ironically. He kisses Sylvia and Adrienne. Rinette and Émile-Paul accompany him to the apartment door. Adrienne kisses Rinette, thinking that her sister doesn't look too bad, all things considered, but then Émile-Paul's illustrations, of naughty nuns and fellating aristocrats, will always find a market even in times such as these; perhaps particularly in times such as these.

Sylvia and Adrienne clear the table and wash the dishes. They remark on Valéry's quiet courage, his refusal to collude with the Germans, even though, as one of France's greatest living poets, pressure has been applied. They drink a last cup of chicory together then, just as Sylvia is moving towards the door, Adrienne asks her what the German officer looked like.

'Well…' Sylvia describes him then looks intently at Adrienne, sensing a fresh wave of perturbation. 'Is anything wrong, Adrienne?'

'Everything's fine,' Adrienne replies gently. 'Go home and sleep, dear one.'

Sylvia regards her silently for a moment; then they kiss. Adrienne watches her slip across the street to her apartment, an inky shadow barely rippling the darkness.

The night-walker

It is almost midnight when Adrienne sits down at her desk. There is something appropriate about the time because she is about to make an eleventh hour appeal. She has forgotten, once again, to draw the curtains and she stands in the doorway, looking out at a sky which is Prussian blue and cloudless. The streetlights in Paris are now dimmed by paper shields; the city is dark and the stars clearly visible. Adrienne takes no pleasure from them. Unlike the sky above her parents' village, the stars' presence here seem unnatural and only serve to underline the changes which have taken place.

She crosses the room, twitches the turquoise-coloured curtains shut and switches on the lamp. She uncaps her fountain pen then reaches into her desk for some coarse pages. (Léon-Paul Fargue describes the quality of the Occupation paper as 'shitty', fit for one activity only.)

My dear Victoria
    I'm writing to you about our good friend Veronique. As you know, Veronique is fond of travelling and July, last year, she took a train from Paris to the countryside. For some time, she has been staying with her friend Marianne in a lovely room with a view of the local vineyards.

Adrienne puts the pen down. She's not even sure this communication will reach its destination: as far as letters go, Occupied France is sealed to the outside world. However, she knows a lot of people, and, although the Germans do their efficient best to supervise the movements of the population now in their power, it's an impossible task. A way will be found. It must be found. She remembers the telegram, delivered the day after the Occupation began – *Say if safe am with you all*

– Victoria's concern reaching across the mountains and the ocean from Argentina

> However, I think her time in the countryside is coming to an end and she would like to leave Marianne and travel on alone. Veronique enjoys sailing and she hasn't been eating very well lately so I believe she would find a sea voyage beneficial for her health. I recall your kind invitation issued some years ago, your offer to put your house at her disposal. There are wolves near the house where Veronique is staying and at night these make her uneasy...

Adrienne stops again, crosses out the last few words. Literature is her life: she has published the work of some of the greatest writers of the age, has even contributed in a small way by publishing her own stories and poems, but she is finding this letter a greater challenge than anything she has ever attempted. How can she outwit the censors yet still convey her meaning? Of course Victoria, cultivated, sophisticated, will know that 'Marianne' is a reference to France but the rest of the letter seems clumsy, liable to lose its meaning in transit. Victoria's vast fortune, made by her family on the Argentine pampas, will be put unhesitatingly at Adrienne's disposal, if only Adrienne can convey the real measure of Gisèle's peril.

Adrienne rises from her desk and paces restlessly around the blue-papered room which she usually finds so congenial. There is the white-on-white embroidery, a linen cloth worked by Rinette; the Lalique vase patterned with blue irises which was a tenth anniversary gift from Sylvia; and the rosary beads beneath the statue of the Virgin Mary which both belonged to her father's mother. There are none of Émile-Paul's pornographic watercolours on the walls, although there are a number of his portraits, executed in pencil.

And there are photographs, including one of Adrienne sitting at her desk reading, taken by Gisèle. Gisèle gave this to Adrienne shortly after they became lovers, when Sylvia had returned briefly to the States, in order to have her troublesome womb removed. Stressed though she is, Adrienne smiles when she looks at her 1935 self, absorbed, unaware that she is about to fall prey to the all-seeing Leica.

Next to her portrait is a dusty oblong of wall where once Gisèle's 1938 portrait of Walter Benjamin hung. After he died, Adrienne couldn't bear to look at it but his visitation earlier that evening has restored something in her so that now she retrieves it from the top of the wardrobe and returns it to its original place. Walter Benjamin gazes back, using his right hand to shield his face, immortalised one afternoon in the Bibliothèque Nationale. Gisèle had caught something, Adrienne thinks. If she had never known this man, she would have guessed by looking at this image that he was often a refugee from reality, sexually blocked and overly cerebral.

'Photographs are like ghosts,' Gisèle had told her once. 'They lack substance but carry the imprint of what once was.'

Adrienne gazes back at the chubby, bespectacled face. You always knew what to say, Walter. Help me.

Just as she sits down at her desk again, something lands against her window, making a light, cracking sound. For a mad instant, she thinks it's a bullet. Fear makes her sweat then she hears a familiar voice down on the street. There is a torch beam, like a yellow rosette, which is abruptly extinguished. She peers between the curtains and in the gloom below Adrienne makes out the blockish figure of Léon-Paul Fargue, standing in the dark, surreptitious as an illicit lover.

She raises the window. 'Are you insane?' she hisses.

'Very likely.'

'What are you doing here?'

'Paying you a visit, of course.'

'We missed you at dinner.'

'Ah, well…'

It is pointless remonstrating with Fargue, the night-walker, whose travels take him all over Paris. He may have been drinking Veuve Clicquot at an aristocratic salon or throwing back rough red in some dive frequented by criminals. Like Gisèle, Fargue finds all humanity interesting.

'So, what have you to report?' Despite her irritation, Adrienne wants to hear everything.

'I saw Chanel out with her special friend in a big black car.'

All Paris is aware that the famous couturier, ensconced in the Ritz Hotel, is having an affair with a high-ranking Nazi.

Fargue's face shines like a round white moon below Adrienne as he sings: 'There was a big black pussy in the car, there was a big black pussy in the big black car. Oh, soldier, do you want to stroke my pussy? It's expensive but very chic!'

Adrienne laughs and the knot of tension inside her unties. Fargue is a Holy Fool, necessary because his absurdities so often contain the truth. Who else would find this way to describe the narcissistic collaborator? His lunacy is as necessary as Valéry's very different type of language.

'I could come up, entertain you some more.'

'I've got other cats to whip.'

This expression, similar to the English 'I've got other fish to fry', makes them laugh some more.

'Please go away.' Adrienne loves Fargue but sometimes he wears her out. Adrienne quite understands why her sister's relationship with him is strictly part-time and, occasionally, volatile, although Rinette will never give him up. (How do they manage it, the three of them; but it seems to work.) Adrienne has been known to stay awake until dawn, copying down whatever Fargue chooses to compose, but tonight she is not in the mood.

But instead he throws her a line from a poem he wrote to her sister, years ago. They go back and forth, alternating lines until they join together in the last stanza:

> The organ spoke of shadows…
> On the altar the blue day hung.
> Through wounds in stained glass, the call of the breeze
> Fused with a loud hum of onyx, drove the fire
> Of the candles toward you, tipsy
> With light and sacred songs.

There is the sound of a car further down the street. Fargue vanishes around the nearest corner. Adrienne drops the window and draws the curtains, hoping no local busybody has seen.

She sits down and finishes the letter. She folds the paper and slides it into an envelope as she reviews the events of the evening.

Her anger at Sylvia's omission has disappeared. Adrienne feels no guilt about her affair with Gisèle but she knows how deeply hurt Sylvia was on her return from America to find her place usurped: she can be forgiven her small unconscious act of revenge. (After her initial shock at the changed situation, Sylvia had regained her usual cheerfulness, had even dined with Adrienne and Gisèle in the apartment which she had once shared; then she stayed in bed for a week, vomiting, blinded by her worst migraine ever.)

Adrienne hadn't been able to help herself. Gisèle had brought light and heat to her life. The erotic tension which had always existed between them had ignited during their quest to find Gisèle a husband so she could legally remain in France. (André Malraux's amateur dramatics, 'We must save Gisèle!' had turned out to be just that; as usual, all the work was left to Adrienne.)

'I'd marry you myself, if I could,' she had joked one afternoon, after yet another potential suitor had announced cold feet.

She and Gisèle had been standing close.

Gisèle had turned, kissed Adrienne's neck then bitten it hard enough to leave a mark. 'Not in either of our lifetimes.'

They had finally found Pierre Blum. Shortly afterwards, Sylvia had left for the United States.

Adrienne recaps her pen and tidies her desk, which is always burdened with piles of paper, journals and books. Who would have thought that a chance meeting in the Café de Flore seven years ago would have such consequences? She had gone to have a drink with Fargue who, true to form, didn't show. Breton had been there, hectoring and bullying as usual, surrounded by his sleazy sycophants. A group of them had come rushing in, shouting about nothing in particular, and had crashed into a young woman with luxuriant black hair and broad, almost Slavic features.

'Mademoiselle, they are beasts trampling flowers,' Adrienne had said, helping her to her feet, but Gisèle had been quite unfazed, not intimidated at all, rather interested and amused.

She went straight up to Breton and asked if he would sit for a portrait and later photographed him holding his pipe and looking suitably pontifical.

Here is a survivor, Adrienne had thought, even before she heard about the flight from Berlin. Walter Benjamin had once remarked wryly to her that 'the Third Reich is a train which does not leave the station until everyone is on board'. Like Walter, Gisèle's Jewishness had barred her from boarding so she had taken a different train, across the border and on through Strasbourg to Paris.

There it is again, the faint trilling sound Adrienne heard when she was preparing the meal. She tilts her head first on one side then the other but the noise persists, distant, mutant, on the edge of pain. Eventually it stops. Relieved, Adrienne sits quietly, drinking in the silence, then from another drawer of her desk takes out a small bundle wrapped in aqua silk. She has spent so much time dwelling in the past; now she wants to be a seer. She flicks back the silk, takes out the tarot cards and spreads them across the desk. With great deliberation, she chooses two.

After the exchange with Fargue, she half expects to turn up the Fool but instead draws the Tower and the Six of Swords. She stares first at the image of the fortress riven by lightening then for a longer time at the card which shows a woman setting off on an ocean journey.

Adrienne has a sudden premonition: her voyage with Gisèle has been a great adventure and, if they both survive the war, Gisèle may return to France. But she will not come back to this apartment. The loss Adrienne feels with this recognition is different to the one she feels about Walter or James Joyce or Virginia Woolf. It's more personal; her pride is involved. Events made Gisèle a piece of flotsam stranded on the beach of European history. Adrienne has helped the survivor survive but this has come at a price. Gratitude often breeds a certain resentment, a desire on the part of the one rescued to be free from moral indebtedness.

Adrienne gathers in the cards, shuffles the deck thoroughly, then rewraps it and puts it away. She must accept what is to come as best she can and go on. The Buddhists are right: everything changes. She feels suddenly, deeply tired. The clock on the shelf above the unlit fireplace tells her it is Christmas Eve. Yes, it is time she slept.

But first, a bedtime snack. She goes into the kitchen and takes out the remains of the chicken, tugs the pope's nose from the carcass and chews the piece of fatty gristle with pleasure, thinking that, for tomorrow at least, there will be a good picking for Sylvia and herself.

Mona Lisa's moustache

A week later and two days before the year's end, Sylvia sets out on her bike, searching for food. Hunger gives her mind a knife-edge clarity in the cold. She wheels left out of the rue de l'Odéon into the Boulevard Saint-Germain then crosses the Seine, now a sheet of ice, and sails into the eighth arrondissment via the Place de la Concorde, yellow registration tag rattling against her rear mud guard. The fog has lifted; the sun is a distant orange glow, a frozen nova on the ice. The wind spikes her blood and lacerates her cheeks.

An ancient Renault, its roof disfigured by the charcoal-burning contraption which citizens use these days, comes crawling out of a side street. Sylvia swerves easily around it and pedals on, overtaking all pedestrians. Cyclists are road royalty now there are so few cars. She passes a nun wearing clogs and zooms on.

The shop windows along her route flash blurs of crimson, yellow and blue; they still display their santons, the colourful wooden figures traditional at French Christmas. However, they hold very little else. Sylvia manages to purchase a last wizened apple at a fruit and vegetable stall bereft of everything except rutabagas and mouldy onions.

She travels on, thigh muscles straining, turns left into the rue St Honoré but at the first intersection the road ends abruptly, blocked by a wall of cinder bricks and sandbags.

A policeman strolls into the middle of the road and holds up his hand. '*Un moment, madame.*' He notes Sylvia's sturdy boots (a pre-war American gift from her elder sister Holly, and a blessing in this glacial winter) and looks with curiosity at the leather motorcyclist's cap with earflaps that she wears.

Sylvia, arrested in mid-flight, wants to swerve around him and sail like Pegasus over the barricade which, she realises suddenly, is higher and more substantial than anything the Germans usually erect when they want merely to divert traffic. Behind the wall, in the distance, she sees soldiers, as well as more gendarmes. Something's happened.

Sylvia has not thought it possible to be colder than she already is but she suddenly remembers she is close to the street where the Gestapo has its headquarters.

The cop plunges his hands into her basket and rifles its contents, holding up the Maigret novel by George Simonen which she is currently reading. He flicks through it, smiling a little, as though enjoying the descriptions of gun-toting gangsters and their heavily lipsticked molls. 'So, you like detective stories?'

'Oh, yes,' says Sylvia. 'I'm a great reader.'

'I myself prefer Jean Kery.' The man in uniform continues his search but finds nothing more than the apple, the stubs from some Metro tickets and Sylvia's wallet. 'His books are longer and contain more complex plots.'

'He's a very prolific author,' replies Sylvia politely, then, emboldened by this fragile literary connection, she asks what has happened.

The man purses his lips. He becomes once again a petty custodian doing his masters' bidding. He is medium height and slim with small features, dark hair and brown eyes. If he was out of uniform, you would pass him on the street without a second glance. 'There's been an incident, madame.' He takes out the wallet and checks Sylvia's identity papers, checks the bike's registration tag then waves her away northwards, towards the Boulevard Haussmann.

This annoys Sylvia because it means a detour into the ninth arrondissement, past shops containing goods she can only dream of buying. Nevertheless, she allows herself to feel optimistic about the morning's events. All over Paris recently, red V signs have appeared on walls, bright as feral winter flowers. Perhaps, now, someone has attempted something more daring than mere graffiti. As she cycles east, she thinks about the policeman; she wonders if he ever questions his obedience to the invaders. Perhaps he's a decent family man, only concerned about the survival of his loved ones.

Where is the moral borderline which separates self-preservation from the willingness to actively inflict harm? The tribalism of family, the tribalism of country; take them to excess and they become murderous, destructive.

These thoughts occupy Sylvia as she stops and buys potatoes, encrusted with greyish dirt, precious as diamonds. There's nothing else available that can be had with ration cards; everything else is controlled by the criminals who run the black market. She sets off, intending to share her booty with Adrienne.

As she crosses the Pont Neuf, she sees a bloody V scrawled on one of the bridge's neo-classical columns, as though someone had paused momentarily in mid-flight, or scribbled it under the enveloping cover of darkness.

Sylvia feels a surge of elation. Despite the hunger and uncertainty she experiences daily, she has no regrets about remaining in France. When the war broke out, both her sisters had pleaded with her to return to America. Cyprian, that tragic ex-actress, sacrificed to her mother's loneliness and never-ending emotional demands, had been at first cajoling, then histrionic.

Sylvia didn't contemplate it for a minute. Her adopted country had given her freedom and purpose: this history outweighed any feelings of loyalty she still felt towards the one of her birth.

Snow begins to fall as Sylvia nears her home; the wind gathers force and whirls the flakes, which melt and dissolve as soon as they hit the ground, into treacherous grey slush, causing the bike to skid. Sylvia almost falls, the puts her head down and battles on, thinking of hot roast potatoes.

'Pommes aux potassons!' she shouts. She tries it in English: 'Potatoes for *potassons*!'

When she rounds the corner into the rue de l'Odéon, she feels a little like Ulysses, an epic traveller returned. She halts outside Adrienne's shop. Her breath is a steamy cloud as she wipes snow from her eyes.

Then she sees the car, black and panther-sleek, waiting outside Shakespeare & Company.

Immediately, Sylvia U-turns across the street and props the bike. She doesn't stop to plan or strategise, she tries to think calmly as she walks but this is impossible. Her assistant is alone with a predator.

Since Jews were excluded from university study, Françoise spends more and more time at the shop, even though there are so few customers. Sylvia remembers the day Françoise learned she had been accepted, her face lit up as she rushed into the shop, waving the letter from the Sorbonne like a flag of victory. Her dream of becoming a renowned scholar of Oriental languages and history ended, she is no longer that bright, forward-looking girl. She has become withdrawn; her clothes are drab, her hair lacklustre. And now she is face to face with one of those responsible.

Sylvia sees his trim graceful shape through the window. She pushes open the door.

'*Bonjour, madame.*' He regards her quizzically, boots highly polished and uniform immaculate.

Sylvia returns his greeting, more tersely than she intended. He smiles.

She goes to stand next to Françoise, who is sorting the morning's mail. A sharp smell rises from the young woman's rust-coloured blouse. Sylvia touches her hand, which Françoise retracts, her expression sullen.

The man advances, holding a small black beetle which Françoise has missed in her daily sweep and dust. As he pinions her with his eyes, he slowly pinches the insect to death between thumb and forefinger then drops it onto the table next to the stack of mail. 'You need to get rid of this. *Vermine* are best destroyed.'

He turns his attention to Sylvia again. 'I've come about the book we discussed at our last meeting.'

'It's been put away.' (Actually it's no longer in the shop but Sylvia realises telling him is pointless.)

He moves closer, ten inches taller, crowding her. Sylvia stands her

47

ground, meeting his eyes, hoping he can't hear her heart. 'It's been put away.'

'I have given you every chance, tried to be reasonable. You've chosen not to cooperate. We'll be back later today, to take away your books.' On his way out, he glances briefly at Françoies then stops once again in front of Gisèle's photographs. 'You have some very undesirable friends.'

He goes out the door, closing it quietly and walks to his car. It moves slowly toward the Boulevard Saint-Germain then disappears.

'Fetch Adrienne,' Sylvia hisses, 'and don't come back!'

Françoise flees across the street like a young whippet to number eighteen.

As soon as she is gone, Sylvia leaves the shop and rushes upstairs to the apartment above her own, where the building's concierge, Madame Grise, has her lair. This is the way Sylvia thinks of it because the apartment always exudes a faint meaty odour, from the soups and stews Madame concocts for her large extended family, who are frequent visitors. Sylvia knows that her status as a foreigner and a member of *les intellectuals* renders her suspect in her concierge's eyes; now, their long relationship, cordial, if slightly wary, is to be tested.

Madame Grise, when importuned, is not enthusiastic. Sylvia beseeches, she implores but it is not until she mentions the possible destruction of books by French authors that the widow gives reluctant consent.

'*Je suis une patriote, madame*,' she says, with a long-suffering sigh, as Sylvia trundles her down the stairs, just as Adrienne arrives, followed by her assistant.

Maurice Saillet leads a small trolley, pulling it along as though it were a pony ridden by a much-loved child. 'Can't this wait for a few days?' he asks.

'No,' replies Sylvia shortly. 'It can't.'

For a moment, all four survey the shop contents. Bizarrely, Sylvia thinks of a miracle story she was raised with, the feeding of a vast crowd with five loaves and two fishes. The same air of impossibility hangs over the enterprise before them.

Then, as always, Adrienne begins. 'Boxes,' she says briskly.

'There are none…'

'Well, find some,' and boxes are found, stacked on the trolley, filled with books then carried up the stairs.

Up and down the stairs they go.

At first, Sylvia pretends she is an elevator operator in a large important department store, transporting shoppers through multiple levels. 'Going up!' she calls cheerfully. 'Ground floor: perfumery, ladies' leisurewear and lingerie. First floor: drapes and manchester,' but eventually she realises that she had better save her breath.

Apart from Maurice, none of them are young and the last two years have tested them all to their limits. Adrienne climbs steadily, never stopping, her breathing slightly louder than usual. Madame Grise is already blowing like an old carthorse on its way to the knacker's yard. Clouds of dust, rising from books and journals untouched for years, hang in the air then lodge in their lungs. Sylvia sneezes repeatedly, remembering childhood days incapacitated by asthma.

'Bless you, *cherie*,' says Adrienne, toiling steadily on.

When there are no more boxes, they heap the books in their arms and continue. Up and down the stairs they go.

Ghosts attend them on these endless ascents, all the people who ever bought books and had been friends of Shakespeare & Company, even if those friendships sometimes didn't endure. Sylvia picks up a shallow woven basket filled with cards and letters covered in writing faded to illegibility, the whole thing wearing rags of dust.

Something falls out of the basket and glides to the floor, silent as an autumn leaf. It's the photo taken of Sylvia in 1919, just as she was setting up Shakespeare & Company, by Lucy Schwob, or Claude Cahun as she called herself then, actor, writer, photographer and infamous and illegal cross-dresser about town. For some time, Claude, shadowed by the faithful Suzanne, her lover and stepsister, had been a regular visitor to the shop and the two women had also frequented Adrienne's. All of which came to an end when Adrienne refused to publish Lucy's book. (This decision had been largely due to economics but privately Adrienne had also considered the book narcissistic and convoluted, too influenced by that self-indulgent movement, surrealism.)

Lucy and Suzanne had withdrawn from Adrienne and her circle, had aligned themselves more and more with André and Jacqueline Breton and their cronies. Sylvia's laugh comes out as a gasp as she thinks about the culture wars of the twenties: how seriously they had taken themselves then. How pointless and irrelevant those conflicts seem now!

She picks up the photograph and replaces it carefully on the basket.

Eventually, they have cleared half the books. Up and down the stairs they go.

Their continual tramping and lifting has lifted a fug of sweaty flesh into the air. Maurice Saillet, after consulting the ladies present, removes his suit jacket and rolls up his sleeves. The back of his white linen shirt is damply furrowed and Sylvia, behind him, experiences a spurt of lust. She imagines the strong supple spine arched above her, as she bites the smooth young chest, the lean ascetic face above hers.

She's amazed by the her sudden fantasy – she, who has never been interested in men, apart from a brief and abortive flirtation with Robert McAlmon, who was not interested in women anyway (although Adrienne has told her about the evening Robert tried to kiss her in a taxi, a compliment she repaid by biting him on the lip).

Sylvia realises that her desire for Saillet is not personal: it's his youth, the fact that he still has more of his life before him than behind him that has caused her temporary hormonal frenzy. (Even now, she can't resist a ghastly little wordplay: 'the vigour of his figure'.) A part of her own life has finished; her response is similar to that of a hanged man who comes as he dies, a last flare of life in the face of extinction.

And there it is: a copy of McAlmon's 1938 *Being geniuses together*, bookmarked by a postcard of the *Mona Lisa,* is on top of the last pile collected by Madame Grise. Sylvia has heard that McAlmon, gifted short story writer and poet, indefatigable champion of avant-garde literature, who left Paris after the 1929 Crash, is now working in the family business in Des Moines, selling cars to midwestern farmers. What a waste.

Up and down the stairs they go.

There's a sudden sound, something between a wheeze and a groan, and Adrienne sits down on one of the lower stairs, shuddering.

'Madame,' Saillet murmurs, as he comes to her assistance immediately.

Adrienne heaves herself up then collapses onto one of the chairs waiting to be packed away, pig-pink and sucking air as though her life depended on it.

'Get a glass of water,' Sylvia snaps to the concierge.

There is a sound in Adrienne's ears like the high-pitched whine of a large insect demented by containment. She says nothing, drinks the water, waits for the dizziness to pass and the world to return. Eventually, despite everyone's protests, she gets to her feet.

'You're no good to anyone with a heart attack,' Sylvia tells her.

'There's absolutely nothing wrong with my heart.'

Adrienne and the concierge finish clearing the paper ephemera, the receipts, bills of sale, library borrowing slips and cash books. Sylvia and Maurice start on the furniture, hauling chairs, bumping them against the stairs then dumping them any old how once they reach the fourth floor. They unscrew the lamp shades, including one of Mina Loy's, an illustrated fantasia on papier mâché featuring antiquarian maps and sailing ships which Mina had sold to Sylvia in 1927. Saillet drags a large wooden carton, an old packing case, into the shop from the courtyard behind it and into this goes anything too useless or wrecked to preserve: the shelf which breaks into pieces when they take it down, the book covers with no books, all the detritus of twenty-two years.

When Sylvia finds the flat black envelope under a chair cushion, she extracts its contents without much curiosity until she realises that she has seen it before. There are photographs, some landscapes and a number of portraits done in the fuzzy romantic style fashionable in the early twenties. There is one of a slender beautiful blonde girl draped with lace, gazing wistfully out of a window.

These are what the teenage Gisèle Freund occupied herself with in Berlin, and what she first showed Adrienne and Sylvia, laughingly protesting their awfulness, then pushing forward a folio of more mature work, her street portraits of workers, raw and direct.

Sylvia recalls how charmed she and Adrienne had been by this in-génue performance (although not taken in by it for a moment), this young woman speaking bad, Berlin-accented French, wearing the dark coat which had accompanied her into exile. Now, Sylvia's tempted to throw them in with the ripped and torn sheet music of Tosca and an eviscerated Bible. (Who did that? Louis Aragon, perhaps?)

Now would be the perfect time: Adrienne won't notice, given the state she's in. No. Sylvia replaces the photographs and pushes the enve-lope into the first box she sees. The photographs stand for something, someone's labour and aspirations and she doesn't wish to denigrate that.

By the time they finish the clearance, it is late afternoon and the light outside is turning to ashes and lead. Saillet, who is the last to make the final descent, comes down the stairs holding something in his hand the way a priest holds a communion wafer. He picks up a pen and makes a small embellishment. The three women, waiting for the tradesmen Madame Grise has called, watch without comment. Now that the shop is empty, their footsteps echo eerily, as though they are walking through a cathedral or a mausoleum. Madame Grise sweeps the floor, scooping trails of mouse dirt into a dust pan. After Sylvia's animals died, first Teddy the terrier, then Lucky, her black cat (a great favourite of Léon-Paul Fargue's), it became difficult to keep the pesky rodents at bay.

The carpenter and painter who arrive are clearly the concierge's kins-men: one dismantles the remaining bookshelves, the other sets up his ladder outside and begins the obliteration of the name painted in 1919 by Émile-Paul Bécat. Adrienne takes down the board hanging under-neath which features her sister's very French-looking Shakespeare, com-plete with twirly moustache.

The painter dips his brush, dips it again. Swish, swish, then it's done.

Sylvia and Adrienne stand outside on the pavement. Sylvia is stunned, numb. Adrienne cries silently.

Inside, Sylvia hands Madame Grise the key and thanks her for her help. She tries to joke, drawing an analogy between their successful move of five thousand books to the biblical feeding of the five thousand. The concierge looks slightly offended at this reference to her Saviour and departs to prepare a meal of her own, to which only her relatives are invited. Sylvia suddenly realises that all through the war the meaty smell has not abated: Madame Grise must be buying on the black market. Possibly, her lack of friendliness is not personal; she's just worried about being reported to the authorities.

Sylvia sneezes. Suddenly, her legs threaten to give away and she leans abruptly against the wall. Adrienne walks over, puts her arms around her. They're exhausted – beyond exhaustion – as they make the final exit. Even Saillet looks pale as he tapes the postcard to the inside of the shop window.

Sylvia locks the door. She collapses against Adrienne and sobs dryly. Passing pedestrians stare at them curiously but say nothing; no one remarks on the shop's changed appearance. Shakespeare and Company has already passed into history.

'You better come home with me, at least for a few days.'

'I'll be all right, Adrienne.'

'No, they know who you are and where you are. There is safety in numbers,' Adrienne says firmly.

Despite everything, Sylvia feels a certain weary triumph. When Gisèle returns to Paris after the war is over (Sylvia has to believe that it will end, that the Allies will be victorious), she will find things changed. Let her find out how it feels to be pushed aside.

Wordlessly, the two of them walk the short distance to number eighteen, leaving Saillet to lock up Adrienne's shop. Sylvia has collected her bike with the precious potatoes and wheels it along. It seems like another year since she set out this morning; another century.

Adrienne lights a small fire and they sit trying to warm themselves at its feeble flicker. Eventually, they rouse themselves to boil the potatoes. Rinette has recently managed to find artichokes and has donated two of them to her sister. There's no butter for the vegetables so they eat them with salt and pepper and drink a red wine which has a lingering vinegary taste. They fall into bed, twined together like children. As she snuggles into Adrienne's bulk, Sylvia's last thought is regret, that she didn't rescue McAlmon's memoir as a 'thank you' for Saillet.

Adrienne looks down at her sleeping companion, sees that Sylvia's features do not relax; glimpses the craggy face of her old age.

Mantle of blue

New Year's Day comes and goes. On the foggy third of January, Adrienne sets off for the fifth arrondissement, a heavy sapphire-coloured shawl draped over her grey vest and skirt. She wishes for flowers, a resplendent bouquet to honour the city's patron saint who she is going to both venerate and invoke this morning. Adrienne left before Sylvia woke; she knows that this sort of activity is beyond her friend's Presbyterian comprehension and anyway Sylvia is one of the reasons for Adrienne's journey.

She walks to the Place de l'Odéon at the end of her street then turns left into rue Racine, which crosses the Boulevard Saint-Michel and becomes rue des Écoles. On her left is the Sorbonne, on her right the Musée de Cluny, which houses the medieval glory of the Bayeux tapestries.

Cold thickens the fog: the clammy air coats everything and reduces her sensory world. As she turns the corner into rue de la Montagne Sainte-Geneviève, Adrienne almost collides with a man in a business suit who tips his hat and murmurs apologies. She hurries to her destination, anxious to be inside. Across the way is the Panthéon, resting place of the distinguished, but Adrienne has no interest in its chilly neo-classical columns today; her business is at Saint Étienne du Mont, the great church begun in the Renaissance and finished as a Counter-Reformation battle cry.

The walk has been less than two kilometres but she's puffing slightly by the time she arrives. How did medieval men and women manage those epic pilgrimages across Europe which sometimes took years? No doubt they were sustained by a stronger faith than hers. She dips her hand, genuflects then walks slowly beneath the vaulted white arches, past the rows of chairs where several people pray. Today is the feast day of Saint Genevieve, patron saint of the city, the admirable woman who saved it from invasion by the Huns almost fifteen hundred years ago. ('What a pity the Hun prefers fighting to fun,' T.S. Eliot had remarked to her, quoting Noel Coward, on the last occasion Adrienne had seen him, reading at Shakespeare and Company in 1936.)

She enters the side chapel where the reliquary which houses the saint's corporeal remains is kept, thinking ironically that perhaps Saint Genevieve has developed hearing problems in advanced old age; but the faithful would defend her, saying that all that had happened was punishment for the godlessness of the Third Republic.

Adrienne lights a candle and stands looking at the statue of the star-crowned Lady in her cerulean robe, this anaemic Christian descendant of the ancient fertility goddesses. It was here, in this very church, that a priest murdered the Archbishop of Paris in 1857, shouting, 'Down with the goddesses!' which, Adrienne thinks, was a rather extreme way of showing his displeasure about the recently enshrined dogma of the Immaculate Conception. This intimate space, with its polished wood, the gleaming brass and gold lit by candle flame and the light received through stained-glass windows, makes her forget the cold. She kneels and prays.

She's always soothed by Catholic ritual, even though her grasp of it is rudimentary. 'Holy Mary, Mother of God,' she mumbles, wishing her free-thinking parents had taught her the proper Catholic words. But perhaps it was just as well: she was not indoctrinated with dogma as a child so she has never felt the need to rebel against it; never entirely embraced it either. She will never copy T.S. Eliot's leap of faith.

Adrienne prays, in spite of this. She prays that her letter has reached Victoria and that soon there will be an escape route for the woman she loves. She prays for the other woman she loves who for the past few days has been drowning in a stupor of depression. She prays for the end of this interminable hellish war and for the liberation of her beaten down country. If Saint Genevieve can't do it, then let it be the Free French.

She opens her eyes and looks into the candle flame, gazing at it until her mind clears and she finds a calm space within herself. Then she rises to her feet, grunting softly. Approaching footsteps tell her that she is about to have company. She looks once more at the glass-sided reliquary which holds a very small container. During the French Revolution, the saint's remains were exhumed, burnt and scattered: there's really not much of her left.

Adrienne drops some coins into a box and walks out into the opaque air. The sun struggles overhead and people pass each other in the streets like wraiths. She wonders what Sylvia is doing and whether she will manage to get out of bed.

Sylvia lies inert beneath the covers as she hears Adrienne moving about, preparing for her day. She realises that the pain in her head which has kept her company for the last three days has subsided to a dull throb. She lies still, eyes closed, hoping that sleep will claim her again, so that she doesn't have to contemplate the day ahead, but her body stubbornly disregards her intention. Her stomach begs for food, her skin craves cleansing.

Adrienne leaves, bound on her errand of faith. Sylvia knows that, for the first time in the years of their relationship, Adrienne is keeping something important from her, something to do with Gisèle. Sylvia is no stranger to divided allegiances – she took her own father's name for her own, yet supported and cared for her emotionally frail and needy mother for years, those two people whose marriage was a battlefield – but she thinks that Adrienne's withholding is a form of protection; and that annoys Sylvia. She is not a child, doesn't want to feel like one. She must have it out with Adrienne.

Silently, she pushes herself up and sits on the side of the bed, legs dangling, then shuffles, zombie-like, across the room to the basin, where she bathes her face. Her vision has cleared, it's no longer a horror movie of flashing black shards, but when she enters the kitchen and pulls the curtain aside all she sees is a white blank, depthless and featureless. She shivers, sits down abruptly. Her blood feels sluggish, congealed. Adrienne has left out croissants but Sylvia can't bring herself to heat the clammy, whey-coloured things. She makes coffee, drinks a cup then dresses and goes out into the fog.

The swirling air shields her, offers its protection as she creeps the few doors along the street to her apartment, although it's not thick enough to prevent Sylvia glimpsing the empty shop windows. She averts her eyes, hurries up the stairs. A dank wall of air greets her and she warms herself by moving about, selecting a clean flannelette nightdress and some extra toiletries. Dust has already settled over her books and papers and on the cluster of photographs arranged in her sitting room. There's Sylvester, there's Eleanor, dead in Paris by her own hand, a secret Sylvia must take with her to her grave and keep from Holly and Cyprian, the sisters she hasn't seen for years. So much loss: Sylvia is suddenly immensely exhausted, feels as though she is walking on an alien planet where gravity pulls her down. She barely manages to make it to the bed.

When she wakes, she lies wondering where she is, her limbs stiff and cramped. After a few moments, she rises, almost falls but manages to reach the door. She feels completely unmoored; the world is a tilting dangerous thing: she must reach sanctuary. She stumbles down the stairs into a street which is cold but clear and only just avoids knocking over a man, out for a weekend stroll with his family, who glares at her as he shepherds his wife and three children past. He thinks I'm drunk, thinks Sylvia, and laughs aloud, compounding his belief.

She lets herself into number eighteen. Where is Adrienne? Sylvia tries not to imagine a fall on the slippery pavement or some random criminal attack. She walks down to *La maison des amis des livres,* thinking Adrienne might have called in to chat with Saillet.

Adrienne, turning safely into the rue de l'Odéon a few minutes later, sees the long black car pull up outside the vacant shop. For a moment, she freezes then pulls herself together, bypasses her apartment and walks sedately to *La maison des amis des livres,* where she signals soundlessly to her assistant and Sylvia. From their vantage point across the street, they watch the German irritably order his driver to bring a torch from the car.

'The Fritz is getting annoyed,' Saillet remarks with satisfaction.

'Gerhard. His name is Gerhard,' Adrienne says softly.

Sylvia glances at her sharply but her attention is diverted by the officer, who thrusts the torch beam through the window, probing the shop's interior. But his spike of light finds only dust and the postcard of the *Mona Lisa* which Maurice Saillet has left taped to the inside of a window. As an inspired afterthought, he has adorned the image using one of the many pens he always carries: the most famous face in Western art wears a Hitleresque moustache.

At the moment, very few people know where the painting is. The Louvre's curators emptied the museum of most of its treasures in 1938. They are stashed in crumbling provincial chateaux, except for the most priceless pieces, including Leonardo's masterpiece, which the curators keep on the move, circulating them so efficiently that they are kept out of German clutches. The postcard is a tiny taunt, the resistance of the powerless. While Adrienne explains the joke to her, Sylvia wishes that the French military high command had shown as much foresight and organisation as the country's cultural custodians.

They watch the German stab and stab with the torch before he returns to the car. His expression is furious. He motions curtly to the driver. Despite everything, the three onlookers enjoy a small moment of triumph. Sylvia and Adrienne giggle like malicious schoolgirls as the car slides down the street.

'He might come back.'

'He won't.' Adrienne takes Sylvia's arm. 'Come home.'

They invite Saillet to drop by after he finishes in the shop, then they walk up the street together. The temperature has continued to drop and before morning it will snow. They discuss Saillet, his courtesy and helpfulness; Adrienne mentions that they could not have done what they did earlier in the week without his assistance.

'He is our new young *potasson*,' murmurs Sylvia, then, setting her mind against the image of the dead shop and its graveyard of books above, says, 'I must go back to my own place tonight.'

'Why?' Adrienne unlocks the door of the apartment.

Sylvia is silent for a long time. 'I must have courage,' she says at last. 'Life goes on.'

'How profound, darling.' Adrienne kisses her lightly. 'Let it go on here.'

What Sylvia won't say, she has too much pride, is that she fears being supplanted again, that sometime there will be another usurper. No, even living beneath a graveyard is better than that.

'At least stay to dinner,' Adrienne says pleadingly and Sylvia glimpses the burden secrecy imposes, the unwanted confinement of privacy.

'Of course.' She must trust Adrienne will share whatever she has on her mind when she is ready. Sylvia can wait; but she will not give up her apartment.

They settle down companionably for the rest of the afternoon. Sylvia finishes reading *The madwoman from Itterville* and Adrienne writes a short essay about a recent lunch she enjoyed with Colette.

Later, they turn the last of Sylvia's potatoes into a floury soup; Adrienne sets down bread, tasteless stuff probably made from wood shavings. Maurice Saillet joins them later, carrying a bottle, the contents of which they make jokes and guesses about: 'lighter fluid', 'paint thinner'. As they sit down to eat, a shadow passes imperceptibly across the window. Outside, a young girl, dark-haired and pencil-slim, wearing a flowered frock beneath a sea-green coat, crosses the street. Ice-blue light veins the sky.

Le passeur

Paris, March 1942

Adrienne battles her way through sleet the evening she goes to meet the smuggler. The water gives the cobblestones a treacherous glisten and the hem of her long grey skirt flaps soddenly against her ankles. 'Spring-time in Paris,' she mutters ironically.

The weather exacerbates her feeling of disorientation, brought on by being in this seedy and unfamiliar part of the city. She had wanted to meet in a place both more comfortable and public, believing that clan-destine activity is best conducted in the open, but her contact had been unyielding, insisting on this destination in the fourth arrondissement.

Adrienne has lived in Paris for over thirty years. She thinks she knows her city well yet it constantly surprises her. Nondescript alleyways can open onto small parks or squares featuring a statue of some minor eighteenth-century dramatist whose stone features are crumbling, the plinth beneath his buckled shoes moss-encrusted. There is no such En-lightenment relic to be found in this squalid maze.

Sylvia, the only person who knows that Adrienne is bound on this mission, warned her about going alone and advised against it. 'At least let me lurk around in the shadows.'

'No, I can't afford any complications.' Can't afford to get lost either, Adrienne thinks, as she stands holding Sylvia's navy blue umbrella which a sudden squall of wind almost turns inside out. The map she drew five days ago, after her contact told her the address, slips from her fumbling hands onto the street. Water swells and blurs the blue ink lines and arrows then fades them to oblivion.

Adrienne curses softly. She really wants to scream or roar but can't afford to draw attention to herself. There's a bar ahead; she will risk exposure and ask directions there. She wills herself to stay calm, tries to remember what was on the map but it was drawn in haste and stuffed into a skirt pocket. Nothing comes back. At least she will be out of the weather for a time and perhaps have a chance to warm herself.

As she approaches, several Arab men come out of the bar. There's a car coming towards her down the narrow street, blocking her way so she can't avoid them. Adrienne stands back against the wall trying to look as inconspicuous as possible. The men speak African-French, so Adrienne does not catch hold of what they say as they look at her and laugh. She recognises the tone, denigrating, meant to dirty. She does not meet their eyes as they brush past, one leaning into her breasts. She waits until the men are silhouettes at the end of the street, hugging the small cloth bag concealed beneath her coat to her body. She waits, mute as a victim, until they are gone because she must not lose Victoria's money.

The bartender is a small man with olive-gold skin and a black goatee beard. He addresses a group of Arabs in their own language then inclines his head courteously towards Adrienne and greets her in French. Before she can ask for assistance, he pours a small glass of clear liquid and sets it down before her. 'Drink, madame.'

Adrienne thanks him, wraps the glass with shaking hands then downs the contents, which taste like petrol. It's probably Eastern European, an unlikely kind of drink for a place like this or perhaps some desperate wartime concoction distilled illicitly; whatever its provenance, it does the trick. Warmth forks her body and her trembling stops. And she is not really lost: all she has to do is continue to the end of the street, turn right and proceed for three blocks then turn left.

The wind has dropped and the rain eased to a curtain of drizzle. Adrienne peers ahead, sees a stray dog shit then skulk off. She holds up her skirt, carefully negotiates the heap of steaming ordure. She passes shops bearing the yellow sign: *ENTERPRISE JUIVE*; most of them are empty.

Adrienne feels for the cloth bag. She knows that there has recently been a round-up, that there is a giant holding pen in the suburb of Drancy where human beings are yarded like cattle. There are rumours about trains to the East; some think that the Germans will build a special prison on the outskirts of Paris. Nobody knows anything for certain.

There are no streetwalkers but as she turns into the street which is her destination, Adrienne notices a furtive gleam of red light. She thinks that this is the sort of area where poor women come for abortions. Criminals, dark-skinned immigrants, strays of all kinds: here is the social detritus that the other residents of the city choose not to think about. Two Germans pass on the other side of the street, coming from the brothel, ordinary soldiers who cannot frequent the higher class establishments.

She stops before an apartment building located over a leather goods seller, looks for the wooden staircase on the outside, then takes a small torch from her coat pocket: she's not taking any chances as she climbs the slippery five floors. She folds the umbrella, grasps the shaky hand rail. She is a heavy, earthbound woman with wet hair, poised precariously on rickety boards above a cesspool. By the time she reaches the top floor, she's panting; she does not look down, knows if she does the street below will spin. There is a door with a heavy handle of rusted metal before her.

She knocks loudly then, after waiting about fifteen seconds, knocks again. A voice instructs her to enter.

'Rathole': that is what Adrienne thinks when she enters the small windowless box with dark grey walls, filled with the reek of kerosene from a heater on the bare wood floor. Behind the heater, a man sits at a flimsy table, the type people often play cards on. In the corner of the room is a single bed with another chair next to it. Everything is neat, Spartan, the corners of the blankets tucked in with hospital precision, and there are clothes folded on the chair. The room is as clean as it can be kept, although the ceiling is darkly stained. Adrienne looks for a small picture of Marx, or Lenin or Stalin but of course there are none because the organisation to which her host belongs is outlawed.

He regards her for a moment without speaking, a stocky man of medium height with curly dark hair, round brown eyes and oddly small chubby hands. His feet would be white and delicate, Adrienne thinks irrelevantly, feeling suddenly that she has wandered into a scene from *La Bohème*, this man looks so much like an Italian tenor, which is closer to the truth than she realises: he's the son of an immigrant from Arezzo who came to this country just after the First World War. The son was a boy of twelve, not long left school, old enough to go to work, old enough to see that his family were treated no better in this country than their own.

He greets her tersely, tumbles the clothes onto the bed and produces the chair. 'Sit, please.'

Adrienne hands him the cloth bag. 'My good friend Antonio is bringing you a present...' ran part of Victoria's accompanying letter, which Adrienne had burnt as soon as soon as she had read it. She has no idea how Victoria had contrived this risky transaction. (Years later, she will learn that the money was carried from neutral Argentina by a merchant seaman Henri Michaux had befriended during his travels in Latin America.)

She watches the money being counted, the precious money which will buy the forged documents Gisèle needs for her escape; some of it goes to her host's party. Adrienne accepts that the payment is necessary; she also sees that the man before her, taciturn, ideologically driven, will not betray her. She is not sure that they are fighting the same war, not exactly; nevertheless, they have a common enemy in the Germans. Adrienne has heard of cases where smugglers contract with the desperate, only to lure their prey over the border demarcating the Occupied Zone and Vichy, into the hands of the collaborators. No, whatever this man is, he is not greedy. This thought gives her the courage to attempt some kind of personal contact.

'My friend is Jewish. She was involved in anti-fascist politics in Germany before 1933. You may have seen her photographs in *Life* magazine in 1936, of the English unemployed…'

'Yes, yes…' He gestures impatiently then rises, walks to the door and swings it open, bringing in a gust of grey sleety air. He motions Adrienne towards it. 'I will be in touch with your contact when I have made the necessary arrangements. Until then, do nothing. Try to live as normal a life as possible.'

It is on Adrienne's lips to say that in no sense of the word could the life they have been all living for almost two years be called normal, but she decides against it. She listens as the man directs her to the nearest Metro station.

'It's open…' he continues, forestalling her question, for since the Occupation began dozens of stations have been closed; the Germans worry about what goes on underground.

Adrienne gets to her feet, hips and knees protesting, head dizzy and stomach nauseous from the kerosene fumes. The rain falls unrelentingly but so anxious is she to be gone from these surroundings that she's halfway down the stairway before she realises that she's left Sylvia's umbrella propped behind the door.

For the second time in the evening, Adrienne curses but she won't turn back now. Inadvertently, she glances down and the street blurs and skews. Adrienne feels as though she is descending into a vortex. By the time she reaches street level, sweat soaks her chemise and beads her hairline. She desperately needs a toilet. She hurries to the end of the street, away from the man of granite and the blemished vacant shops.

The street narrows abruptly, until it is little more than a passageway, a medieval leftover which has escaped several generations of urban improvers. Adrienne glimpses a sheen of light against the dark walls ahead, prays that she will not meet anyone deranged or malevolent coming the other way, prays that her bladder will hold out; then bursts through to a phantasmagoria.

Well, it is really a small dilapidated cinema with a nearby *bar-tabac* but Adrienne feels like a wanderer returned to civilisation. The cinema is showing a lightweight romantic comedy starring the blonde actress Danielle Darrieux. Pure escapist trash for a difficult time; and perhaps people are grateful for the chance to sit somewhere that's heated. As the doors open, Adrienne notes the size of the emerging crowd. Most of the seats must have been occupied. She slips in to use the convenience, feels an almost erotic relief as the liquid gushes out. She remembers visiting her parents at Rocfoin, all the long country walks she has taken with Sylvia, when all you had to do was squat behind a bush. She wishes she was there now.

She washes her hands, attempts to repair her sopping hair then rejoins the people outside on a pavement littered with sweet wrappers and cigarette butts. She moves with the crowd towards the Metro, never noticing the man with red hair wearing a long navy coat and dark muffler following her.

The space underground is cavernous and cold; beneath the harsh lights its pale yellow tiles shine with an antiseptic patina. (The Germans seem paranoid about contagion; everything over which they have control gets cleaned thoroughly.) Adrienne takes up a position on the edge of the waiting herd. The cigarette smoke and the stale odours which drift from some of her fellow travellers have make her nausea return and she sways slightly, willing herself not to vomit.

The train comes purring in on its rubber wheels and she waits as people crowd forward then moves in the direction of the penultimate carriage, seeing the sullen faces of Senegalese passengers, now segregated at the rear.

'Animals at the zoo,' Adrienne hears one laughing young man remark about them to his girlfriend, who also laughs.

Adrienne steers past them and slides into the last available seat. The red-haired man enters the carriage just as the doors close and walks past her to the end, where he stands holding a folded copy of *Paris Soir*. Adrienne closes her eyes; the dampness of the heavy coat has permeated her other clothes and she begins to shiver. There is a distant thrumming in her ears and the blood suddenly curdles beneath her skin. If she doesn't reach somewhere warm soon, pneumonia may claim her. As the train crosses the Pont Neuf, she focuses on the other passengers to distract herself from discomfort.

Across from her sit two young German women, their unpainted faces epitomising their Führer's ideal of well-scrubbed womanhood. They are clerks, or stenographers, support staff to the uberlords, who must surely never be tempted by these stocky prim girls who might otherwise be hausfraus in Bavaria. Adrienne feels a sudden spurt of national chauvinism when she compares them to a French girl sitting nearby, talking animatedly to her boyfriend. This girl is obviously poor, some put-upon milliner or shop assistant with little education, but next to the two dowdy frauleins, she shines like a star. She has rouged her lips vibrantly and her cheeks delicately and wears what Adrienne can only describe as an insouciant hat, a dark red felt button on the back of her head with a little veil. Adrienne takes pleasure in her, as she often does with young women, appreciating their beauty and liveliness.

Gisèle was twenty-six when she and Adrienne met for the first time. She had never worn anything as remotely feminine as that wicked little hat but when they had finally gone to bed, she and Adrienne had barely left it for three days; had almost broken it. Adrienne's chuckle dies to a sigh. She closes her eyes once more, hoping that the man to whom she has given all that money, and who now holds Gisèle's life in his hands, will get good use from Sylvia's umbrella.

In his apartment, Dmitri de Luca listens to the fat woman's descending footsteps, waiting until their sound is swallowed by the rain. He hopes she won't fall; he doesn't want to have to deal with her blubber on a night like this. He sees the forgotten umbrella but doesn't run after her. If he pursues her, it will send a wrong signal to the man tailing her to the station and then to her home. Dmitri hopes that it isn't that dope André, conspicuous even apart from his ginger hair, but they have lost so many comrades lately, some of their best men have been executed, that they cannot pick and choose when it comes to even routine tasks.

At least the fat woman will only be able to waddle, not run; that should make surveillance easier.

For they cannot afford to take chances: people write letters to the authorities denouncing their neighbours for petty misdemeanours. Behind the mask of decent, everyday Frenchmen and women are those only too happy to turn in their countrymen for breaches of curfew and ration restrictions. How much more satisfaction would these people gain to hand the Germans a real enemy, one of the hated 'reds'.

This has happened. Trust no one.

Everyone seeking assistance, who wants a parcel carried to a relative in Vichy or an escort across the border, away from the Germans, must be treated as a potential trap. Dmitri believes that the fat woman is genuine, thinks he may have heard of her beleaguered friend, this social democrat who photographed the unemployed English. He has no time for such people, who are willing to make deals with the bourgeoisie to gain parliamentary power, who seek to pander to liberal sympathies by showing workers as objects of pity. In some ways, they are more dangerous than the fascists; at least you know where you stand with them.

Pictures do not change history; only mass action does.

He puts the money given to him for the Jewess's passage to safety in a small locked box which he hides beneath the floorboards – not a very original place but it's the best he can do in this rathole. He uncaps a bottle of beer and pours a glass, a self-indulgence he rarely permits, then lies back on the bed.

He's worried about his son Viktor, safely sequestered in Vichy with his mother Paulette, and her mother. The boy's ten, at an age when he should be leaving the influence of women; too much time around them will make him soft.

Dmitri sips the beer, remembering the week the three of them spent at St Malo in 1937, the first paid holiday, courtesy of the Popular Front government. He had made a sandcastle on the beach with his son, then eaten fried oysters wrapped in newspaper with Paulette. Most days it was too cold to swim but they had walked on the grey sand, Paulette bare-legged, shoes in hand, light brown hair tousled by the breeze. She had wanted to return the following year but by that time Comrade Stalin had signed the pact with Hitler. Doubting people, those who could not comprehend Comrade Stalin's tactical genius, had left the Party (Dmitri had even doubted too, for a short while). At a time of such confusion and disarray, there had been no time for holidays.

Dmitri finishes the beer then goes out into the night. It's Tuesday: he has a standing arrangement with the local brothel, a sullen teenager off an impoverished farm in the Auvergne who services him. It's purely practical: Dmitri thinks of it as something similar to scratching an itch and after he empties himself into her, his mind is clear and he walks back to the room, glad that the rain has finally stopped.

Tomorrow, he will begin to organise the false papers for the Jewess. Dmitri frowns, as he pauses briefly before a vacant besmirched shop which once housed a kosher bakery, disregarding people moving past in couples and groups from the local cinema. The Jews are always a problem. By their very stubbornness, they don't ask for trouble, they sometimes sit up and beg for it. He also doesn't understand why they don't organise, don't fight back. They lie down like sheep, line up before the authorities so they can be tracked like hunted animals. The rich ones, of course, have got away; but rich people are always able to do that.

Dmitri moves on. It doesn't pay to linger anywhere. He will help get the Jewess out of France. The rest of the money the fat woman gave him will be used for bribes and guns. He tugs his jacket around him as he climbs the stairs. The stars now visible that the rain has cleared look down without sympathy but he expects none. When the war is over, he wants to walk on the St Malo beach again. Until then, his survival skills honed in the Spanish Civil War, and the strength of the party, must be enough.

When Adrienne alights at Odéon station, she has what she realises is a Proustian moment. Coming up into the air of the street, away from the fetid train with its detritus of cigarette stubs and torn tickets, she catches the first hint of spring, the merest warm breath borne above the smell of charcoal and wet pavements. Bulbs will be thrusting up determinedly in the Tuileries and the Jardins des Luxembourg (where the bronze replica of the Statue of Liberty still stands; the one in Bordeaux has been seized by the Germans and melted down). Soon, flowers will open and the long grey days surrender to sun.

It was on just such an evening two years ago, the last spring of freedom, that she and Gisèle had crossed the Boulevard Saint Germain, on their way home from a concert given by Monique Haas, who had played Bartok and Ravel. En route, they were greeted by Francis Poulenc, Henri Michaux and two American French-language students, all of whom had, in the course of their conversation, thanked Adrienne for some assistance she had recently rendered.

Gisèle, who had been twitchy and irritable all evening, had stood by, silent and disconnected, watching the faces of the crowd coming up the rue de l'Odéon from the theatre. 'You're such a handmaiden, Adrienne,' she had remarked, after the students moved off towards the Metro, 'always doing good for others.'

Adrienne had started to laugh, wanting to make some risqué pun on 'hand' and 'maiden'; then she realised that the comment was not intended as a compliment. 'Oh…' she had said lightly, not wanting to show how stung she felt, 'then what do you suggest? Always doing bad?'

'You know that's not what I mean. What about the writing you never have the time to do now because you're always doing things for someone else?'

Gisèle was referring to the poems and stories Adrienne had published, under a pseudonym, many – oh so many! – years ago. These small works of fiction had been well received, even praised – until the author's real identity was discovered. Then the tide of critical acclaim had, quite markedly, ebbed.

'*Cher* Adrienne,' Valéry had said, taking one of her hands in his, his nicotine-stained index finger gleaming yellow as a poisonous star, 'we would miss you too much if you sat in your apartment all day writing novels.'

And that had been that. Gisèle was right: no one had helped her; no one had given her the support she had gifted countless others.

'I believe I'm more like a midwife than a handmaiden,' she had said, still trying to deflect the argument she knew Gisèle wanted. 'And perhaps all artists need those: people who promote them, lend support. There's nothing wrong with helping people, and, heaven knows, I've done my share of helping you, organising the exhibition, printing your thesis…'

Her words had trailed off as she forced her anger down. She understood that the woman walking next to her, swinging along in her dark coat and beret, was a driven egotist. Certainly, you could never accuse Gisèle of being anyone's handmaiden. The crowds of theatregoers had dissipated; the rue de l'Odéon was quiet. Adrienne reached for her lover's hand. She made the risqué pun she had first intended and Gisèle laughed.

By the time they reached the apartment, they were reconciled, had drunk coffee and eaten pieces of a sumptuous cherry tart Adrienne had made that afternoon while they listened to a recording of Schubert's 'Gretchen at the spinning wheel'. Later they had slipped beneath the duvet and made love; however, looking back now, Adrienne realises that the scene on the street was the beginning of the end.

As she turns into the same familiar street alone, Adrienne feels old, cold, tired and depressed. The wet coat weighs her down and there is a tingling behind her eyes which she suspects is a prelude to fever. So, she has been out helping Gisèle again and will probably catch a chill for her trouble. But it had to be done: even if Vichy's anti-Semitic restrictions are not tightened (and Adrienne believes the iniquitous bargain the collaborators have struck with the Germans will not last), Gerhard von Eckersdorf is too close. So helping Gisèle has not been a choice.

'Adrienne!'

She looks up from her reverie to see Sylvia approaching, the in-evitable cigarette in her right hand. Just the sight of that glowing tip is enough to warm Adrienne.

They kiss in the formal French way, cheeks touching, lips puckering the air. Sylvia hugs, in her informal American way.

'I've lost your umbrella,' Adrienne says, by way of greeting.

'No matter.' Sylvia pulls a face as she feels the wet coat. 'I've got a fire going. There is tea – with sugar! – and toast.'

Ah, the elemental poetry of those words, Adrienne thinks as she un-locks the apartment: 'I've got a fire going.' At the moment, no tran-scendent utterances by any of the writers she admires could sound so good.

'Thank you.' She regards Sylvia for a moment. 'You always take such good care of me.'

'I'll always be your clingstone beach.'

Adrienne laughs at the old pun, which she probably first heard in 1921, then she kisses her partner in midwifery. She sometimes thinks about her aborted fiction-writing career, that road not travelled, but as she stands next to Sylvia, remembering their various triumphs as well as their failures, *Ulysses*, the other books and authors discovered, the thousands of readers guided and advised, illuminated, she can't regret the road taken. Midwife: it's an honourable, an essential, profession.

She changes out of her wet clothes and warms herself before the fire's meagre flames. Sylvia hands her a cup of tea.

Adrienne takes her time, sipping the hot sweet tea in its delicate blue and gold china cup and eating the toast spread with a kind of hor-rible gelatinous gruel which passes for jam. There's no butter but she makes the best of it and eventually is sufficiently revived to relate her story.

'You know that Gisèle was involved in anti-fascist politics during her time at university in Frankfurt…'

'Yes.' Sylvia recalls the cold windy evening in 1935 when she entered Adrienne's shop to find the young *émigré* in front of the stove. 'They tried to galvanise people's opposition to Hitler by printing and distributing leaflets.'

'Among other things.' Adrienne sips her tea. 'There were twelve in the group, including a young woman called Elsa. She and Gisèle were very close but Elsa was killed on the day that an anti-fascist demonstration turned violent and the rest of the group were rounded up and put in goal. Gisèle was the only one who escaped. Someone warned her and she was able to catch a train…'

'…taking only her toothbrush and some negatives she had shot at the demonstration,' Sylvia finishes, rather impatiently. She has heard all this before.

'What you don't know – Gisèle only confided this to me later…'

Sylvia flushes. She knows what 'later' means.

'…is that she believed the group had been infiltrated.' Adrienne breaks off to pour them both more tea. 'Or perhaps this person started with a pure heart then, for some reason, went over to the National Socialists. Anyway, the group was betrayed.'

'And you think this literary officer, the one who came into the bookshop, was responsible?' Sylvia looks sceptical.

'He's the Judas, yes. Your description fits a young man named Gerhard who was the unacknowledged leader of the group. On this particular day, the day of the demonstration, Gisèle saw Gerhard in conversation with two Brownshirts.'

'Well, that doesn't prove anything.' Sylvia puts out her cigarette, lights another and inhales. 'He was probably in confrontation with those thugs.'

'Gisèle seemed to think not. "Involved and intense" was the description she gave – but she only glimpsed him for a moment, before some of the Brownshirts' comrades saw her with her camera and gave chase.'

'Well, why would he be interested in her now? Surely his comment in the shop was just an idle one.'

'She is the one who got away. And she's Jewish: that's enough. And the film Gisèle smuggled out of Germany, which she has never developed, did show people being attacked and beaten. She told me that. So you see, my darling, it's important that she no longer remains in France.'

Adrienne pours more tea. She knows it is time for a change of subject. She tells Sylvia about her travels through the Marais, the dark shuttered shops and the man with the cherubic face and sentinel eyes. They both find comic relief in her account of finding relief in the rickety cinema. Eventually, Adrienne, so tired she can barely think, allows Sylvia to guide her to bed.

Two weeks later, Dmitri de Luca climbs into a coffin lying in the back of a sleek black hearse behind an undertaker's business in the eleventh arrondissement. It's a good quality coffin, one of the best models the business sells, and his unshaven face is kissed by the plush satin lining as he settles down. The better the quality, the less likely the fascist authorities are to suspect a hoax. The driver carries all the correct paperwork for a recently deceased bourgeois. Dmitri has with him his own false papers and a revolver.

A few minutes later, the lid is clamped down. There is a soft scratching sound as something slides along the top. This is the wreath of white lilies, placed carefully below the ornate gilt cross. A Catholic cross, not the Russian Orthodox one Dmitri remembers from the hours spent with his mother in churches as a child. She had worked as a maid for a family of minor aristocrats until she caught the eye of Salvatore de Luca, the gardener they employed at their summer villa in Biarritz, in 1908. The family returned to Moscow, without Tatiana, and were all killed ten years later. Tatiana mourned them; her son thinks their deaths were a historical necessity.

He lies in the darkness, seeking the single small tunnel of light which will tell him he has air to breathe, then hears the car's engine cough to life. As the hearse trundles slowly south through the Paris suburbs, he passes his hand over the white satin lining and hears, just above his head, a faint crackling sound. One of the female comrades, she organised the strike at Chanel's couture house in 1936, has unpicked part of the fabric then skilfully resewn it, hiding the documents intended for the Jewess.

Women are useful sometimes, Dmitri thinks, although if the Germans or the collaborators across the border take the hearse and its contents apart, he's done for. No matter; he has the revolver, purchased, along with some others, with part of the fat woman's money. It he's discovered, he will at least take someone with him, as payment for Comrade Semard, General Secretary of the Railwaymen, who was executed last week. If he reaches his destination safely and meets the Jewess at Our Lady of Perpetual Succour as arranged, he will make his way back to the Occupied Zone any way he can; on foot, if necessary.

Dmitri is a veteran of the Spanish Civil War. He's used to hardship, walked for two days without sleep or food, walked until the rags around his feet wore out and they bled as he and the rest of the battalion retreated from Teruel, walking, walking, walking in the cold, while the German and Italian bombers roared overhead. Swimming the Loire River and hitching lifts to Paris will be easy, compared to that.

He lies in darkness and remembers the civil war, the best and worse time of his life. The camaraderie which soured when the stupid Anarchists continued trying to do things their way; the generosity of the Spanish people which turned to desperation (before he left in October 1938 he had seen women offering themselves for bread); the continued refusal of the Western democracies to aid the Republic, scared shitless that the interests they were bent on protecting would be nationalised. There are men he knew who now lie rotting, coffinless, beneath Spanish soil.

Dmitri believes that their deaths were not in vain. After the war is over, there will be a popular uprising. A Communist government in France will be established. The party will get rid of the bourgeois nationalist, de Gaulle. All collaborators, great and small, will be dealt with.

He moves restlessly. The air in his hiding place is stuffy and there is a pressure in his chest, as though a strong man has placed his hand against it and is pushing, rhythmically and unrelentingly. There are hours ahead yet but Dmitri wills himself to stillness. He has a mission and, after it, other business. Killing business. He banishes all thought, focuses on the image of the tulips he saw as he made his way to the undertaker's this morning, their tightly furled scarlet slits heralding the new season.

Part Two

South of France/Spain

A small place

South-west France, April 1942

'You should know about lighting candles,' says Elsa, that gentle teaser; she is entirely aware that her friend Gisèle is ignorant of the rituals of her faith. They are two girls, blonde and dark, Christian and Jewish, who call themselves, jokingly, Marguerite and Shulamith.

The university basement room is cold. In the centre of the circle of chairs a solitary flame flickers, its dark twist of smoke blown about as the door to the rooms opens and shuts. Tears of wax melt and congeal at the mouth of the Chianti bottle in which the candle has been placed.

'What, Elsa, are you trying to turn this place into? An Italian restaurant? That would be most inappropriate.' Gerhard's greeting is jovial, brotherly, trying to cover his true feelings, so betrayed by his actions, always volunteering to help her, always wanting to be near her. In the leaping, dancing shadows, his hair is rich as a fox's pelt; his greenish eyes hold twin fires.

Elsa laughs, not at all put out.

Johannes smiles, jumps up and hugs her, then kisses her cheek. 'Don't pay any attention to him.' He shakes Gerhard's hand vigorously then hugs him too.

There is a circle of faces, all twelve of them now, laughing in the umber glow before things get serious and talk turns to the demonstration next week…

…where she has scaled the statue of Goethe in the main square of Frankfurt so she can better look down on the crowd surging like a river, blood-red banners against a grey sky, but there is no use trying to capture that brilliant spill of colour with the film she is using. Everything will be

monochrome: the front of the seventeenth-century houses, white; the clear
sky, pale grey (she has forgotten to bring her yellow filter again); darker grey
for the various complexions of the demonstrators, although the two little
girls in the foreground will look ethereal as angels...then there are the two
Brownshirts who see her camera and they are chasing her, they want her
film, they will stop her at the border and prevent her reaching France...

When Gisèle wakes, sweating and shivering, it is not long after dawn and slivers of light pierce the painted shutters. Past the window which faces out onto the street drift the sweet thin voices of children singing *Marchele, nous voilà!*, the song honouring Vichy's octogenarian leader, as they walk to school.

Gisèle forgets the dream, only remembers waking on similar spring mornings in Paris to her lover's hands, turning towards her with sleepy arousal, touching her face, her neck, pillows of flesh, while a grey Parisian morning crept across the rooftops. After sex, she would make coffee, carry the deep earthenware cups to the bed on a tray. She and Adrienne would lean against each other companionably, discussing the day which lay ahead, kept company only by the sound of occasional footsteps along the rue de l'Odéon.

As the slanting light falls on the rug in the room in Saint-Sozy, Gisèle hears noise from the kitchen and knows that she will soon have to face the housekeeper. She swings her feet over the bed's edge and pads down the passage to the bathroom, where she runs water in the sink and sponges herself all over, wishing that there was time for a proper bath and worried that she will begin to menstruate today. The mirror above the washbasin shows her pale with bruised skin beneath her eyes and a protruding clavicle, a caricature of vitality.

Back in the bedroom, she folds a clean cotton rag into her underwear then pulls on the new dress, black, patterned with aqua and dark green. She bundles and ties her hair. The house's thick, seventeenth-century stone walls resist the sun, the air is still cold, but when she flings open the shutters, she feels a burst of warmth upon her face.

The design woven into the old rug is a faded mimesis of the bright beds of spring flowers in the street outside. In the distance she sees the tree-covered hills which mark the beginning of the forest. She will miss this – the variegated beds of snapdragon, the open bloom of roses, and the moss-covered stone seat beneath the big lime tree where she has often sat reading – but it is all she will miss.

Before she leaves the room, she closes the cupboard door where the small suitcase stands then makes her way along the passage to the kitchen. 'Good morning, mademoiselle.'

For there is Mademoiselle Devereaux, dressed in her customary black and grey, her grey hair plaited and coiled, the gilt crucifix, a first Communion gift from an uncle four decades ago, at her throat. Her long nose is moist (Gisèle always expects to see a small knob of mucus gathered at the base) and her knotty pewter-coloured eyes glisten eagerly as she places the brioche and watery coffee on the dining room table.

'You are ready for your journey, madame?'

Gisèle replies that she is.

'The hens have laid. I could, perhaps, prepare an omelette.'

Mademoiselle Devereaux has some sort of shadowy family life in the nearby town of Souillac, of which Gisèle remains only subliminally aware. She tries to imagine it as she declines the offer (the thought of the browned edges curling in lard makes her queasy). One of the parents would be a bully; the other browbeaten; a large family, perhaps a brother who got too close: Mademoiselle Devereaux, no doubt the youngest daughter, tyrannised and plain, would have turned gladly to the comforts of religion, might have hoped for a vocation, but perhaps even the nuns could smell neurosis. One of the chief irritants of the last twenty-one months has been the housekeeper's anxious hovering, her insistence on conveying the details of the various maladies with which she is afflicted, but there has been no escaping her: Mademoiselle Devereaux comes with the house. Its owners, friends of Gisèle's parents, insisted that she be retained and that her silence about the identity of their new lodger be bought.

During the last month, this claustrophobia has increased; Gisèle's regular visits to the local church have caused Mademoiselle Devereaux to anticipate a conversion: increasingly, her conversation has fixed on religious concerns.

Gisèle chews the brioche, which is covered with some kind of ersatz yellow goo, and drinks the unsatisfactory coffee. 'I do like a woman who enjoys food,' Adrienne had said, on the afternoon of their first meeting. Well, in order to enjoy food, there must be food to enjoy, Gisèle thinks wryly.

In her bedroom, she applies lipstick and knots a cheap, brightly patterned scarf beneath her chin. She glimpses herself in the mirror. She looks ludicrous, a long-faced, hood-eyed imposter, a gangster hoping for absolution.

She picks up the suitcase and carries it to the door, hoping to just call goodbye to the housekeeper, but she is waiting, with something in her hand.

'Madame,' she says tremulously. She holds out a book, its dark blue velour covers worn down to leatherette at the corners, its shabbiness redeemed only by the gold cross printed on the front. 'Please take this with you. Anything which brings you closer to Our Saviour and his Blessed Mother…'

'Well…' Gisèle has told Mademoiselle Devereaux that she is visiting friends in Brive-la-Gaillarde, a town to the north, and will return in three days. How else to explain the suitcase? If she accepts the loan of this treasure, it cannot be returned. She tries to think of some suitable excuse that will not divulge her real plans but nothing adequate occurs to her and Mademoiselle Devereaux has tears in her eyes.

Gisèle murmurs her thanks and takes the book. Opening it, she sees that it is an illustrated *Lives of the saints,* published by Bayard in 1923. There is an inscription in looping sepia ink, *To dearest Camille…*

'I will take the best care of it, mademoiselle.' Impulsively, she embraces the person who has cooked and cleaned for her for almost two years, feels a shrinking inside garments which smell of onions and dust, hears a flustered bleat which may also contain delight.

She walks quickly towards the church, head down, because the village is a small place with many eyes. 'Surveillance': she knows it's a French word which originated at the time of the Revolution. Committees were set up all over the country so that citizens could denounce each other in the interests of ideological rigour. Now, this level of bureaucracy is unnecessary: people happily inform on their neighbours and colleagues without any coercion. Gossip which trickles down through the porous border between the Occupied and Free zones tells her that, in Paris, informing has become a mania, a national sport: now, the whole country is a village.

She approaches a cluster of shops and sees the baker, round-faced, with the high colour which suggests an overactive heart, sweeping the pavement, but they just nod without speaking as she passes. In his front window, a poster of Marshal Pétain, Father of the Nation, patriarch of a reborn Catholic France, looks down on the few trays of available croissants and buns.

Gisèle crosses the street, rounds the first corner on the left and sees the boxy white church with its concave-sided steeple. She hopes fervently that Father Laverny, he of the gentle humour and chocolate-brown eyes, is not there. During the course of their conversations over the last month, she has come to like him and it's been increasingly difficult to maintain a facade of theological interest when all she is doing is wasting his time: her visits to the church must appear as though they are made for a reason so that her presence there on the day of her departure is not questioned. Gisèle has tried to think of her biweekly meetings with the priest as a game, necessary to her survival; nevertheless, she is glad the pretence is over.

She dips her hand in the font and genuflects in the dimness. The early Mass is finished; only one woman remains, clicking her rosary. The newcomer sees with relief that this elderly parishioner is far to the rear of the church, away from where she herself must sit.

She takes up her position in a pew beneath the sixth Station of the Cross, the one which depicts Saint Veronica wiping the face of Christ with a cloth. She watches the flickering of the lighted candles, the motes of dust which drift in the multicoloured shafts of light thrown across the altar by stained glass. A scarlet splash vivid as blood causes her to seek its source and, gazing upwards, she sees Judas, his hair aflame against the sun, watching Christ break bread, surrounded by the other disciples. 'One of you will betray me...' She remembers long ago in Berlin, standing next to her father, as he tells her about the drama in the Garden of Gethsemane. Looking back, she understands that Julius, in an oblique way, had also been trying to teach her about anti-Semitism but she had been too young to realise it.

Gisèle opens *The lives of the saints* and turns the pages, fine as old skin. Various scenes of gore and decapitation flick past until her gaze comes to rest on a depiction of a pretty young blonde carrying her eyes on a plate.

This is Saint Lucy, a virgin martyred in the fourth century for giving away her dowry to the poor. The man to whom Lucy had been betrothed was annoyed by this act of charity and informed on her to the Roman authorities, revealing that she was a member of a proscribed cult. After numerous persecutions, including having her eyes gouged out, she was put to death by the sword.

Gisèle gazes ironically at the illustration; she has never understood Christianity's obsession with sexual abstinence and physical mutilation. However, she does feel a certain kinship with Saint Lucy, victim of persecution and deprived of vision. Boredom, as much, if not more, than fear, has been her constant companion since she fled from Paris. (She had tried to get a job working in the darkroom of the only photographic business in Souillac, had produced her portraits and photojournalism to show the owner, only to be told that he could not run the risk of breaking the law by employing a Jew.)

Yes, being deprived of your eyes is torture.

She reads on, past the phallic impaling of Saint Sebastian and the trials suffered by Catherine of Siena until her own limbs cramp and her fingers chill in their inadequate cotton covering. After a time, she feels so conspicuous that she kneels, breathing the musty odour of sanctity, a smell of dust and stale incense which lulls her to drowsiness. Through half-closed eyes she watches the candle flame…

Elsa wears a red sweater beneath her coat when the group meets on the evening before the demonstration. Gisèle is slightly late, rushing from a tutorial with Adorno and when she enters the room, she is aware something has changed although everything appears as usual.

Gerhard stands in the centre of the circle of chairs proclaiming strategy with Johannes's eyes fixed worshipfully upon him. 'Little brother,' Gerhard calls him affectionately, although they were only cousins, sons of brothers who are both eminent lawyers in Frankfurt.

It is the look of triumph which Gerard throws her which makes her heart lurch and then she sees the expression on Elsa's face as she watches him…

There is a soft click as a door closes.

Gisèle feels another cramp, this one in her lower belly, familiar and unwelcome, and has just realised that she has started to bleed when there is a muffled sound as someone settles into the pew behind her.

'Excuse me, madame, can you tell me the date of Saint Veronica's feast day?'

'July the twelfth,' she replies, without looking around.

Seconds go by; she sits still as a graven image, watching the candle-light, then the voice resumes.

'Wait five minutes before you leave. There is a van parked across the street. Meet me there.'

If she wasn't afraid, Gisèle would be amused by this *Boy's Own Paper* aspect of the assignation. As it is, she waits until her watch releases her then walks along the grey-carpeted aisle, carrying the suitcase.

As she comes out of the church, she is momentarily blinded by the brightness of the day and stands there blinking, an earth-dwelling crea-ture emerging from its burrow. When her eyes focus, she sees the small truck, with the dent in the driver's door and its black paint faded to charcoal. She can't see the voice which spoke to her.

Then a man jumps from the rear of the vehicle and extends his hand for the suitcase. 'Get in.' He stows it, unlocks the cabin, curses softly as the van resists his efforts to start it, and eventually wrestles it onto the road.

They cross the Dordogne, dark green water oiling its way past the village, where a solitary canoeist glides placidly. It is still possible, for some people, to engage in everyday pursuits, to behave as though nothing has happened. Gisèle looks sideways at her companion, sees the jaw burred with stubble and the soft sag of skin beneath. While she waits for him to speak, she lights a cigarette, draws in the smoke which makes her so dizzy that she is back in the Romanisches Café on the corner of the Kurfürstendamm, having her first at seventeen.

'Please wind down your window.' Her driver's tone indicates that it is not a request.

Gisèle winds the window right down, letting in the draught which even the slow-moving van creates. She is pleased to see that his jaw tightens, although he restrains from commenting. She winds it right up again until there is a hair-crack of air while she smokes; then lowers it to halfway.

'You have things I need, monsieur…'

'Don't speak. We'll stop when the road enters the forest.'

Dmitri de Luca's self-control, severely challenged by the Jewess's adolescent antics, solidifies once more as he drives her south. He glances back but sees nothing behind or ahead which is cause for alarm, just a normal flow of traffic which includes farmers with horses and carts. His whole progress on this mission has been uneventful but his passenger, this scarecrow in the shoddy rayon dress (even in these straitened times Paulette would never let herself look such a fright) puts him on edge.

He is glad when they reach the forest and begin to wind upwards, through strands of young oaks.

Gisèle sees the flinch and shudder of light through the maze of leaves. She has been a banished person for almost ten years; she has begun to think in French. Increasingly her own language, that corrupted tongue, eludes her. Now her mind clutches at a word which slithers away, flails just out of reach but is eventually pinned down. *Waldeinsamkeit* – 'the feeling of oneness with the forest' – the word surely a thread of race memory from the pagan past, solemnised and given new life by the Romantics.

When she had first come to Saint-Sozy, she had sometimes thought about running away to this place and living in a cave, knowing the idea as a fantasy of sanctuary, an illusion connected to the times spent as a child in the Tiergarten, playing hide and seek with her brother under the eyes of servants, or later, walking with her father. (Mutti, that hothouse flower, never ventured outdoors unless she had to and even then, only to shop at Wertheims and Hermann Tietz.) There had been a time when she was eight and her brother was eleven. He was always pinching and shoving;, they were out of sight of their father, running through a grove of trees, and he had forced her down then straddled her. She had drawn back her arm, felt an elastic thrill as her fist connected with cartilage. She remembers the screams and blood, the punishment which followed (although its details are lost to her).

The car reaches a side road and Dmitri de Luca drives some distance then stops beyond the gaze of houses (for even here there are cleared encampments of civilisation; the forest is pitted with tiny villages).

From beneath the seat he takes a large envelope which he hands this to his passenger. 'Please inspect these. You need to familiarise yourself with your new identity.'

The woman stares at the passport, the French exit visa, an entry visa to Argentina and a certificate of good conduct from the police. They tell her that she is Veronique Baudin. There is the ticket to Argentina, bought with American dollars, more precious than blood. She stares at the photo in the passport, an old one Adrienne must have rescued from somewhere. Four years have been taken off her age; she hopes she can pass for twenty-nine.

My name is Veronique Baudin.

The driver passes her Vichy money, notes and the dull grey coins inscribed with *Patrie, Travaille, Familie*, which always make her want to wash her hands after she has handled them. 'If we are stopped by the authorities, I am your brother-in-law…'

'A relationship which seems almost sufficiently removed, monsieur.'

'…and we are on our way to the market at Cahors.'

'And what is our cargo?'

'Carrots, mademoiselle. Carrots, potatoes and turnips, but mainly carrots. What else would we be carrying?' He gives her a thin smile. This, together with the veiled reference to Vichy's failed agricultural policies, is his first and last attempt at humour or friendliness. He turns the car round and they resume their journey.

Gisèle closes her eyes, hopes the rag will hold her flow. It would be humiliating to have to ask him to stop somewhere so she can change it, although worse to have to wash blood from her dress when they reach their destination. The trees loom on either side; she sees a rapid flapping of light as they pass an injured bird which lifts its wings uselessly by the side of the road. Overhead, a hovering merlin waits, calculating prey with its black razor eyes.

This is how she had felt sometimes, roaming the Berlin streets, the lens of the Leica a third eye; like a raptor, a bird of prey waiting to pounce. There was a power, fearlessness, that having the camera bestowed, made her more than an untidy teenage girl (although there had been the time when she had had to run for her life from an angry pimp not happy at having his livestock recorded).

You are raised in a life of privilege, brought up to expect that it will flow like a strip of negatives spooling smoothly through your hands, sequential images held up to the light but then your father loses a lot of money in the Inflation and that lovely life becomes jumpcuts, awkward splices with all meaning disrupted.

Best thing that ever happened to me, Gisèle thinks, squinting into the sun. It made me grow up, took me out of my destiny to be a hot-house flower (although I was never pretty like Mutti). It made it easier to demand education, too: nobody wanted to marry a poor girl, not the sort of boys I'd been raised for; so I had to do something. Going to that high school, in a suburb where I'd never been before; I met Elsa and the other girls. Nothing hothouse about any of them…

…going with Elsa to the Eldorado Club, laughing, egging each other on, exhilarated and scared by turns. Elsa, the beauty with yellow hair halfway down her back bribing the tough old dyke on the door, flickering candles set on tables at which women sat wearing collars and ties, their arms draped around their girlfriends dressed in silk and crêpe de chine. She and Elsa dancing, holding each other and giggling, not daring to do any more. In the early morning, as they made their way home beneath a blurry white moon, there was a man and a woman fucking against a wall, blatant as cats; men dressed as women selling themselves in alleyways, the whole sideshow that was Weimar…

When Gisèle wakes the driver tells her they are approaching Cahors. She glances across, sees his hands (with surprisingly clean fingernails) steady on the wheel. What is his life, then? She would like to know. She is good at drawing people out. She recalls that when she was preparing the portraits for the 1939 exhibition, she spoke at length with Valéry, with Breton and Malraux: men like to talk about themselves. Virginia Woolf had seen the cunning and the patience which ran through her conversation, the gentle interrogation to reach the split second which conveyed the essence of personality. She'd called Gisèle a 'devil woman' when she saw the result.

But these days it is best not to know too much about anyone, in this country which has become a village.

They cross the turreted medieval bridge, enter the town hugged by the U-bend of the River Lot and move steadily though the streets, where every second corner is plastered with a phalanx of posters bearing the Marshal's face.

'This is as far as I go.' Her driver cuts the engine.

While he retrieves her suitcase, Gisèle stands and stretches, noting with surprise that it is barely mid-morning. Before her, the railway station is a grey clangorous space, its enormous machines dwarfing the humans who serve them. During the 1920s, there were certain types of images made fashionable by Germaine Krull, André Kertesz and Alexandr Rodchenko, photographers who had turned soaring slabs of steel into industrial cathedrals and transformed wheels and rivets into stark, sharp-edged modern poetry. Gisèle had admired them for their technical acumen but they never spoke to her, seemed divorced from the human element, the makers and tenders of the machines.

She turns away, looks on the people entering the station, picks out the faces she would like to record: the thirty-year-old with the dirty blond hair and heart-shaped face, once pretty, now worn down and bitter-looking. The older man, prosperous, suited, with a full mouth and large wart on his left ear. She would show each face, warts and all: that is the challenge, letting the personality, and the life, speak to the viewer.

Her eyes rove further, they sift the crowd; then she stiffens, staring at the three policemen crossing the street.

My name is Veronique Baudin.

'Don't watch them. It makes you look as though you've something to hide. Come on.'

Dmitri de Luca has seen them too and curses silently. He wants to get back in the van and drive away but he can't leave her here like this, vulnerable as a wounded bird on the side of the road. He has undertaken this mission and must see it through. He picks up the suitcase, puts his other hand beneath her elbow and steers her determinedly past the flics who have congregated at the station entrance and stand chatting idly among themselves. He doesn't look at them, behaves as though their presence is necessary and entirely expected.

'Light a cigarette and wait here.' He glances sharply at her left hand. 'And take off your wedding ring, you're not married.'

'But I...'

'Do it now!' he hisses. He takes the ring from her and walks towards the ticket booth.

Gisèle wants to laugh. So this is how it ends, the elaborate charade which began six years ago over a chessboard in the Café Mephisto when she told Walter Benjamin she had just been made a stateless person by the German government.

'Get married.'

'What?' Gisèle had almost dropped the white rook in her hand, amazed not just at the idea but that Walter Benjamin should make it, he who never discussed personal matters and barricaded himself against this risk with an almost baroque courtesy.

But, momentarily, the barricades had come down. 'Get married. Find some compliant Frenchman and marry him. That will give you citizenship and solve all your problems.'

'Well, who do you suggest? Maurice Chevalier? Jean Cocteau?'

Walter Benjamin chortled at the idea of the flamboyantly homosexual Cocteau marrying anyone; then regarded her seriously. 'It's what Madame Krull did some years ago when she was in the same predicament as you. She couldn't go back to Germany because of her part in the socialist uprising in Bavaria and she had also been expelled from the Soviet Union. Her ex-lover married her, to give her a home in Holland. It's been very useful to her. Perhaps you could do the same. Find someone…'

And so she had: Pierre Blum, idler, eccentric, man about town, friend of the husband of a woman with whom Adrienne had attended school. Gisèle recalls the wind swirling pieces of grit from the pavement outside the draughty municipal building as she and Adrienne waited for the groom. Henri Michaux had turned up with confetti. 'Surreal confetti,' Adrienne had laughed, referring to Michaux's intermittent association with that movement; but then, the whole occasion had been surreal.

Gisèle waits now, patient as a tethered sheep, right hand folded over her left, feeling strangely naked, until her stubbled escort returns with the ticket. They walk to the platform where the train huffs quietly.

'Please give my regards to your family.' He kisses her on both cheeks.

Gisele smells a body which has not washed for a day but doesn't find it unpleasant. She feels a sudden rush of regard for her surly protector and has a moment of panic at the thought of having to make her way without him. 'What do I do when I get to Toulouse?'

'Buy another ticket, of course.' He turns and is soon a silhouette against the arched entranceway.

She stands looking after him for a moment.

My name is Veronique Baudin.

Then she merges with the crowd moving along the platform.

Towards the sky

At Toulouse there is a problem with the train's engine so she has to wait while the damaged juggernaut is removed then replaced. 'Half an hour,' a station attendant tells her brusquely, so she allows that time plus an extra fifteen minutes (French railway workers are notoriously languid) and goes in search of food and amenities.

She changes her menstrual rag, leaves the other rolled up, soiled and stinking, then walks to a café next to the station, where she orders coffee and a cheese roll. She drinks the coffee but the food revolts her, so, thinking that she might need it later, she stows it carefully. Toulouse is called 'The Pink City' because of the terracotta tiles used in many of the old buildings but as she gazes through the smeared window there is nothing rosy or sweetly pastel in the aspect before her. The light is dull, grainy, making her feel claustrophobic. The people who pass before her wear grey, navy blue and brown.

She must move. She forces herself to rise, leave money, re-enter the world.

As she walks from the café, she passes a public phone and for one wild moment the desire to hear Adrienne's voice, to conjure her physical presence, is so strong that she almost risks missing the train. But she dare not take the chance: if she misses her connection to Bilbao (already in jeopardy by this delay), she will be stranded in Spain. She must not be another casualty, another Walter Benjamin.

This thought, together with her dash through the gates to board (for the shunting and re-coupling has after all been carried out on time) remind her of the day in Frankfurt, 1933, when she had arrived, breathless and harried, to meet him for chess.

'My dear friend,' said Walter Benjamin, looking up from the detective novel he had been reading, 'you appear dishevelled.'

In spite of everything, her narrow escape from mob violence, her doubts about the quality of her afternoon's work, Gisèle had to laugh. She had been running for her life, there was chaos on all sides and all Walter Benjamin could do was comment about her personal appearance.

He opened up the board as she poured out her story.

'I don't know where Elsa is, or any of the others. I've been trying to find them!'

Carefully, precisely, always listening, Walter Benjamin set up black pawns, rooks, knights and bishops, erected his king and queen then looked at her over the rims of his spectacles. 'Your pretty blonde friend has not passed this way and I've seen no one else, nothing out of the ordinary.'

'Well, I can't stay! They're in danger! I'm going back to the university.'

'Then I will have to find another partner or play with myself.'

'Oh, please do! You're so good at that sometimes!'

And that, thinks Gisèle, taking her place in the open third-class carriage next to the window, had been that, at least for some time.

Back at the university, she had run into Gerhard's father, who had frowned, as he usually did when he saw his son's friends. 'I don't know where he is either, but the authorities are looking for you all. For your own safety, young lady, I advise you to leave right away.'

The next place she played chess with Walter Benjamin was one of the shabby émigré cafés in Paris.

As the train lurches from the station, Gisèle gazes around. There is a sign at one end, above the connecting door, which carries a stern injunction not to spit. Across the aisle a young blond man looks out the window. In front of her sit an elderly couple, both dressed in black. Nearby, a younger man and woman, genteelly lower middle-class, in neat but well-worn clothes, speak what Gisèle supposes is a local dialect, one of the variants of Occitan, to their two children.

Over the past two years she has become used to hearing these southern languages. Sometimes it makes Paris and the Occupation seem very far away. Sometimes she has to remind herself that many of these people have never seen a German soldier.

The Toulouse suburbs are as drab as any others: as the train moves steadily south-west, she sees a woman wrestling sheets onto a clothes line and a large dog clamped in a pen three metres square. She shivers because, although the sun is chasing the train, it has not caught it yet. She draws her inadequate jacket more tightly around her and thinks with longing of the English plaid rug she could not pack.

Behind closed eyes she wishes for oblivion which will mitigate her physical discomfort but her mind remains stubbornly alert. She wonders what Mademoiselle Devereux is doing and what her reaction will be when she discovers the subterfuge practised upon her. She recalls the delicacy of Adrienne's skin and the cap of grey knitted silk she sometimes wore. It was a game Gisèle had, a tease, to occasionally sneak up behind her when she was engrossed in reading and release the tumbling pale brown hair from captivity.

The sensual and the monastic: Gisèle had never thought of them as contrasts or elements which clashed; they were both part of Adrienne, integral to who she was.

For an hour, the train toils upward until it reaches Saint Gauden and where the mountains become visible. Rocky tors rear up and behind them are the distant undulations of the Pyrenees. Clouds disappear; the sun strikes showers of silver and crystal from snow. Splinters of light pierce Gisèle's eyes and, across the aisle there is an exhalation, a subtle breath of pain, quickly suppressed.

For the first time, Gisèle looks closely at her neighbour, sees the aquiline features and flushed cheeks. She realises that he is younger than she first thought, only in his early twenties. A bandage around his right hand holds a small dark red seep which has curdled at the edges.

She does not want complications on this journey. Gisèle turns her gaze resolutely out the window, up towards the mountains where, during summer, the villagers graze their herds of red cattle. Peasant certainty: one season follows another; the cattle are driven to the mountains; life goes on regardless of what happens in the wider world. She remembers accompanying Adrienne to her village of origin and meeting her parents. (Although there had been nothing remotely bucolic about Clovis and Philberte; they had even allowed their daughter and her lover to share a bed). For the first few days, it had been strange seeing Adrienne picking fruit or giving her cousin a haircut but Gisèle had gradually realised that it was this practical background that made her a success as a bookseller and contributed much to her persona as a cultivated Parisian woman of letters.

She also saw the constant struggle against nature, and the toll it enacted, noticed particularly the unrelenting drudgery women endured, and had been glad to return to the city.

The sun has caught up with the train and strikes through the window. Despite the increasingly higher altitude, it is now quite warm. Gisèle becomes aware of the moist and pungent odours emanating from some of her fellow passengers, those who live in houses without running water. With difficulty, she prises open the window and then discovers that it drops swiftly as a guillotine blade. Cursing, she wedges *The lives of the saints* beneath it and feels the welcome rush of air through the gap. She hears a sound from across the aisle which could be a stifled laugh. The crash of the falling window has roused him from his slumped position. Gisèle makes a slight grimace, indicates her predicament and he smiles before turning his gaze away.

She realises that this all costs him effort and that his high colour does not indicate health, rather the reverse.

She does not want complications; nevertheless, as the train continues its ascent, weaving around boulder-strewn ridges from which valleys fall away steeply, Gisèle leans across and offers him her roll.

It is a terrible thing, this roll: the bread is made from something Vichy has the temerity to call 'rye' but Gisèle would bet it's never seen that grain. It has been smeared with more ersatz yellow goo and a thin slice of cheese lies sweating in the bread's embrace.

'Non, merci, madame…' He thanks her, says he is not hungry.

He speaks langue d'Oïl, the type you might hear on Parisian streets, from a lawyer or physician. However, Gisèle's refugee ear detects something else, a subtle Teutonic intra-stress on the words, similar to the French-Alsatian she heard as she passed through Strasbourg on her flight from Germany.

Is he German? She thinks not: when she replied to his refusal, there had been no flicker of recognition at her own accent. And why would one of that nation, which has disowned her, be travelling like this? She takes in his clothes, the medium-weight blue suit over a cream shirt with a dark tie. They are good quality but rather worn and slightly too large. This scrutiny she carries out from beneath lowered lids before granting him the immunity of silence.

The sun glazes the skin of her eyes. There is something dislocated, almost surreal about this landscape which Gisèle finds seductive to memory as she falls into a no-man's land between waking and sleep. Later, she remembers this part of the journey as a collection of torn and dirty snapshots found in the bottom of a discarded suitcase…

…Elsa, hair gathered from the nape of her neck, watching Gerhard, her gaze holding a tender sexual submission.

…Gerhard's barely disguised smirk, as he momentarily halts his flow of instructions and gazes back…

…Johannes, looking like a whipped puppy, unloved and unwanted, when he tries to follow Gerhard and Elsa out of the meeting and Gerhard rebuffs him…

…a besplattered, hollow-eyed reflection glimpsed in a train window, as it arrives in Paris on a rainy morning in 1933…

Damaged star

Her breath feels as though it is being strained through a membrane of glass.

Gisèle jerks awake, with the sensation of needles in her blood. They have reached the plateau, are up in the stratosphere, the realm of the angels. The hand she has jammed between the window and the side of her head as a pillow is numb. The air beneath the window gap is silver and sharp. Outside, small clouds puncture pale blue sky. There are trees here which look as though a giant hand has pressed down on them for generations.

She imagines a vast panorama, fertile valleys wrapped by skeins of glittering rivers, a view fit for Eleanor of Aquitaine, but knows that the reality will be another bleak building with bad food and inadequate facilities. Nevertheless, she proceeds towards the exit, corralled between the elderly couple with their large suitcase and the Occitan-speaking family. Boredom has made the children fractious; they whine and pinch one another. Gisèle smiles at their parents, glad that she will always be barren as a rock. She catches the eye of the man in the ill-fitting suit and he makes a small grimace but she can't tell if it is motivated by sympathy for her situation or the pain from his cradled hand. There is a small graze on his forehead, paler than the colour in his cheeks, which she has not noticed before. Perhaps he needs something. She is about to ask but once more he turns his face away.

She tidies herself in the toilet, trying to wash away the grime which seems to inevitably adhere under a reluctant trickle of water and using her tiny vial of Shalimar, an incongruous gift from Sylvia several Christmases ago, to mask the metallic stink of blood. She stands on cracked concrete, drawing in slivers of air. If she could shape shift, she would become a goat, nimble and tough with horizontal pupils in weird yellow eyes, or one of the eagles she has noticed riding the thermal drifts.

She smokes one cigarette, another, and then, when there is nothing left to do, reboards. The seat in front is now occupied by a short, stocky, black-haired man with bad skin and a valise. The hair on the back of Gisèle's neck stands up although this newcomer pays her absolutely no attention. She forces herself to remain where she is; to move away would be to draw attention.

My name is Veronique Baudin. I am twenty-nine years old. I am an artist travelling to Spain.

Her hands steady. She fixes her gaze through the glass.

Towards Tarbes, the air chills and the train descends once more into cloud. There is the outline of trees, pentimento through an opaque mist. Ideas, even emotions, can be like that, Gisèle thinks, as she watches the dark smudges pass by. They can lie just behind a veil of comprehension, not fully understood, and therefore, are destined to remain unexplored or unarticulated. When I saw what had happened between Elsa and Gerhard, I didn't want to acknowledge what it meant for me, what I really wanted from her. So I couldn't go to her and explain that I thought Gerhard might be dangerous, in a number of ways, that his ambition, or recklessness, call it what you will, might do us all harm.

In theory, the group had had no leaders; proceedings were meant to be an exercise in 'Soviet collectivism' but there was a dynamic within which made some members uneasy. Not that this had been a source of concern for everyone.

'Gerhard has such drive and charisma,' Gisèle had overheard Gabi, the only other Jew in the group, say once. Gabi: she had been a plain girl, who had wanted to be Elsa, or at least be in her position. Gisèle had watched Gabi in meetings, had watched Gerhard on that evening before the final demonstration, as he strode up and down in that cellar hideaway, proclaiming his belief that their resistance needed to be more aggressive. This was one of the places wars started, Gisèle thought suddenly: the maiden gazing adoringly at the hero.

But none of these matters had been discussed openly. Public energy was focused on tactics to undermine the regime which threatened them all. Looking back, Gisèle reels in amazement at their arrogance which now seems to her a particular form of political naiveté. It hardly seems possible that there could have been such idealistic people in the world.

Involuntarily, she lets out a small exclamation which is greeted across the aisle by a questioning twitch of the blond eyebrows.

Perhaps it's the earlier sighting of the eagles; perhaps it's nothing more extraordinary than a sharpening of her mind brought on by extra sleep: whatever it is, her memory supplies a crumb of gossip, a half-rumour, overheard as she passed the bakery in Saint-Sozy some weeks ago. *...English airmen...through the mountains...away...away...*

So...this is no German. He's not French either. No, she thinks that this young man, blond, with the eagle face, has fallen to earth like a damaged star. She tries to imagine what it would be like, the Icarus-like plunge from the blazing plane. He must have thought he would die.

Nothing passes between them until they enter the region of those idiosyncratic survivors, the Basques. When Gisèle alights at Pau, she hears a language she can't penetrate, denser than the mist. She walks along the platform which is cut into the side of a hill. It feels subterranean. When she hears footsteps behind her, she waits.

For some moments, they walk without speaking, then she gestures in the direction of the interior and says in English, 'You realise we are not far from Lourdes, where there are many refugees from health.'

'And from sanity, too, I believe.'

Gisèle resists a desire to laugh. 'There must be many people there who pray for the miracle of deliverance.'

'There would be many pilgrims there, certainly.' The wind lifts a lock of hair which has fallen across his marred forehead and he brushes it back. '"Pilgrim" derives from the Latin word for "foreign" but in the times that pilgrimages began, people in the next village were regarded as foreigners.'

Gisèle thinks about her own experience, the constant watchfulness that survival has entailed, constant suspicion that can grow past habit into a mask of madness. 'It is sometimes difficult to trust even those in your own village.'

'Trust is an act of faith,' he tells her, in German. 'A blind thing...'

All Gisèle's hypotheses are jolted out of place, for his German is faultless, better than his French. His French is almost faultless but his German contains the imperfections, the semantic occlusions, of the native speaker. She glances at his profile; if he is who he is proclaiming to be, then she may very well be dead.

He smiles. There is a snide mocking quality to this smile, as though to say, I fooled you. She realises that this blond thoroughbred enjoys playing games and that some of his games have an edge of cruelty. Gisèle is suddenly aware of her darkness, the appearance which delineates her from his own heritage. In another life, he would have disdained her. She hopes she doesn't smell.

Standing on the edge of the draughty platform, she invents his history: read Modern Languages (Classics?) at Oxford, studied at Heidelberg, sampled the delights (only the delights) of the Weimar Republic, reveres German culture: the full Christopher Isherwood cliché. But Gisèle doesn't think he is an invert. How he would have adored Elsa, the butterfly with wings veined with steel, who could, without intention, make Gisèle feel as though she was a dark interloper.

The sun is declining. Greenish shadows settle on the faces of those remaining beneath the bare steel arches. He looks hollow-cheeked and ill.

Gisèle had been intending some sort of riposte, some sort of *who do you think you are* but they are both wayfarers, both pilgrims journeying through the stratosphere, so instead she says quietly, 'It's time to return.'

They sit once more, separately, and she thinks that if she was a believer of any kind, she would pray for the miracle of deliverance, for herself and the young blond warrior. (Elsa had told her about her first Communion, standing in the line of children waiting to receive the

Host at Sacred Heart with her new stockings itching and the tulle veil making her sneeze.)

It's strange what people believe in: the power of a fragment of bread or the curative properties of a spring of water. She still does not know what happened to the small oil print, the *Novus Angelus* by Paul Klee, which Walter Benjamin always kept with him. Since 1921, in whatever miserable room he happened to inhabit, in Germany (after his estrangement from his wife) or Denmark (staying with the Brechts) or the Greek islands or France, there that image could be found. Klee's print had been an icon for Walter, the figure it depicted a messenger from the future: 'This is how one pictures the angel of history... The angel would like to stay, awaken the dead and make whole what has been smashed. But a storm is blowing from Paradise; it has got caught in his wings with such violence that the angel can no longer close them...'

To Gisèle's way of thinking, its flat asymmetrical face always bore a look of mild surprise. She had glimpsed it, hanging above his desk, flanked by pictures of Saint Barbara and Saint Jude, patron saint of lost causes, on a cold November day, when the ascension to power of National Socialists was beyond doubt.

'My dear friend,' Walter Benjamin had said, in response to her repeated exhortations, 'I can't leave. I still have so much to do.'

Gisèle hopes that Klee's work has not been destroyed, that Walter left it in someone's safe-keeping, the same way she entrusted her negatives to Adrienne with instructions that they be burnt if the Germans ever came calling.

She glances across at the injured aerialist but he has fallen asleep, huddled into his dark jacket. The landscape slides past. Houses cling to folds of earth or live in the shadows of stone. The mist clears but the light begins to grey. In the train, dim yellow lights are switched on, which gives everyone jaundice.

The guard comes into the carriage and begins to examine tickets. He speaks affably to the several passengers then moves on to the family group, where he shares a joke with the father and ruffles the hair of the youngest child. His smile is still intact when he speaks to Gisèle but there is something intractable behind his eyes. Beneath the friendly glaze she sees the relentless eternal adherence to every ordinance and pettifogging regulation which is within his power to enforce: the governing characteristic of the French bureaucrat. She remembers hours spent in small stuffy rooms, talking, explaining to men like this, after the Reich had revoked her citizenship and she wrangled desperately for safety.

Despite her best efforts, her hands tremble slightly as she produces the ticket which he scrutinises then clips.

'Thank you, mademoiselle.' He turns his attention across the aisle. Something, is it the bandage, the drape of the fair hair, still elegant though obviously uncombed, make his brows draw together. He turns the proffered slip of paper over slowly. 'Where was this bought?'

Gisèle doesn't hear the reply although she sees the face in profile is calm. The guard, half turned away from her, looks at this passenger then asks to see his identity card.

Gisèle places the tip of one finger beneath the window's blunt blade. With a sharp tug, she withdraws *The lives of the saints*.

Her screams divert the whole carriage.

Gisèle can throw a good tantrum when she chooses. In 1933, on the train travelling to Strasbourg, she had faced down the German equivalent of this official, snapping, 'Have you ever heard of a Jew called Gisèle?' mimicking righteous, anti-Semitic indignation. Oh yes, she can berate and harangue with the best of them: in 1935, she had actually thrown something at the editor of *Vu* magazine when he dared to suggest that she should accept less money for her work than Germaine Krull. ('She has a larger reputation, has been part of major exhibitions…')

Now, Gisèle rents the air with her diatribe and holds up her finger to the guard as if he was responsible for her injury.

'Mademoiselle, I cannot be held accountable…'

'I will seek compensation! I will write to your superiors…!'

'Please, calm yourself!' The guard throws out his chest, begins a condemnatory rant then sees *The lives of the saints* sitting innocuously on the wood-slatted bench, next to Gisèle. Something changes subtly on his face; suddenly he wears a nostalgic expression of someone who has fleetingly sighted an old love after many years. He gives Gisèle a small bow. 'My apologies, mademoiselle. I can offer sympathy but no solution. Perhaps cold water will reduce the swelling. I hope the reminder of your journey will be more pleasurable.' He turns back, clips the young man's ticket and moves on.

Gisèle sits quietly, saying nothing. She keeps her eyes as blank as an icon's while she meditates on luck and chance, recalls the stone-flagged kitchen at Rocfoin with its long wooden table and Clovis Monnier laughing as he recalled his days spent working as a clerk with the railways. 'It's a refuge for all kinds of scoundrels, including ex-seminarians.

Orthez is another town of stone and bridges straddling a river which keeps westward pace with the train and where thick white swirls obliterate detail.

She doesn't look around when she hears him rise from his seat and suppresses an involuntary cry when there is a brief swoop of air and his lips, feather-light, brush hers. She thinks she sees a smudged figure stroll to meet him because, as he disappears into the enveloping mist, he raises both arms, whether in embrace or surrender she cannot tell, so that she is forever left with the image of a strange ambiguous winged creature, hybrid of air and land.

Somewhere, before he reaches the border, he will take his chance like all the others before him, like Walter, who followed one of those rocky ascending trails. How his damaged heart must have strained, struggling to pump blood in the increasingly rarefied air. Walter, that intellectual chess player, so spectacularly ill-equipped for his final journey, had made it through.

But the Spanish had closed the border. To have come so far… Gisèle is certain that exhaustion must have contributed to the decision he then made: the overdose, the end of the road.

She eats the roll, greasy and stale. The quality of the air has changed sublety and she fancies it carries the tang of the sea which she has not seen for almost four years, since she and Adrienne visited St Malo in the summer of 1938. Gisèle laughs as she thinks about Adrienne walking cautiously across the sand then lifting her long blue skirt as she waded into the shallows.

Adrienne would no doubt use the word 'chutzpah' to describe the episode with the window, a word from a language that Gisèle had been taught in childhood was backward and tribal. Her mother, in particular, had disdained Yiddish as a product of the Ostjuden, the poor people currently migrating in droves from Galicia to Germany.

Sometimes we don't need external persecution, Gisèle thinks. We can do it to ourselves although it didn't make any difference in the end, the differences which existed between us. We were all the same, no matter how assimilated, how 'cultivated', in Hitler's eyes. And in France, the legacy of the anti-Dreyfusards had been alive and well.

But not in Adrienne: 'Adrienne is one of the very few French I know not infected with the virus of anti-Semitism,' Walter Benjamin had once told Gisèle at the Café Mephisto, hand poised over the black bishop, pondering his next move. A fitting tribute.

Abruptly, the train halts. First, there is the sound of jostling male voices then, as the first stars prick the sky, several police rush through the carriage intent on some mission known only to them.

Gisèle forces herself to be still. *Don't watch them. It makes you look as though you have something to hide.* Her face is impassive, perhaps slightly bored. She opens the book beside her and reads about Saint Drogo.

Seemingly, the men find nothing. They climb into their car, which merges into darkness and leave abruptly as they arrived. Gisèle reads She does not look up. At a distance, she hears words barked like Morse code. The train jerks, lurches, jerks then lumbers towards the coast again.

Despite the cold, sleep threatens. Gisèle walks up and down the carriage to warm herself and to stay awake: better to be tired than groggy and disoriented at the border. And sleep so often lets in the past and she cannot have that with her now. When she returns to her seat, she heaves up the window, holds it with one hand as she puts out her head to feel the rush of air on her face. The Atlantic Ocean, close now, she imagines as cold and green, an astringent counterpart to the sensual lazy blue of the Mediterranean. She recalls reading Goethe's *Theory of Colours* long ago in Frankfurt; he believed green was the colour of lovers and poets but Gisèle always remembers it as a colour Adrienne disliked, will remember the flare of jealously that lit Johannes's eyes as he watched Elsa and Gerhard leave the meeting together, oblivious to all. *I should have been kinder when he tried to talk to me, should have listened to him that evening but I was too wrapped in my own feelings…*

This is the thought which stays with her as the train crawls on through the night. Asleep or awake, the past damns her.

Sallow & Pudge

Hendaye is the place where, in 1940, Adolf Hitler and Francisco Franco met to discuss Spain's possible participation in the war.

On the platform, people move in slow motion beneath the noon-day brightness of electric light, drained of colour and vitality. Two men sit behind tables at the end of a long shed. Gisèle stands in line, handbag clasped to her chest, suitcase beside her. One of her shoes pinches; the family that was sitting nearby straggles up behind, the youngest child snivelling. One of the men is pale, freckled, with a beige birthmark on his lower right cheek; his colleague is short, corpulent and red-haired. Mentally, Gisèle names them Sallow and Pudge. They peruse, then stamp documents with a bored indifference which only underlines their casual power.

No one is detained. The line inches forward until Sallow beckons. She hands him her passport.

'You travel into Spain, mademoiselle?'

'Yes.' Speech suddenly seems foreign to her. There is a jamming sensation in her brain.

Sallow holds out his hand. 'For what purpose?'

She rummages in her handbag. She hands him the other documents.

He takes his time, pauses over the exit visa. 'So, you are leaving France?'

'Yes.'

'Why?' He looks at her face then at the photographs on the documents.

'I have family in America, parents and a brother.' (They are actually in London, but he doesn't need to know that.)

He stares at her. She meets his eyes calmly.

My name is Veronique Baudin.

A fight has broken out between the children standing in the line behind her. The younger one cries, as does the elder, when her mother slaps her.

'A healthy body needs no fleas,' Sallow says.

'And neither does a corpse, monsieur.' The woman named Veronique stares at him without flinching.

He holds her gaze, seems inclined to speak; then he gestures her brusquely through to where the Spanish border officials wait.

She approaches them with a suitably neutral face, a bland reflection of the one this country now shows to the world. She blanks her mind, does not think of Robert Capa's war photos, the women and children running from bombs dropped by German aircraft; neither does she call up images of the dispossessed pouring into France after the Republican defeat.

She presents her papers, a slight headache throbbing between her eyes, and passes through the border as a lopsided moon rises above the Bidasoa River.

The train, which runs on a narrower gauge rail than its French counterpart, is dirty, the slats of the cheapest wooden seats stained and, in places, broken. Slouched in a corner, numbed to a trance, she watches them fill, knowing her safety is still contingent, in the hands of people who drove Walter to take the morphine he carried carefully across the mountains.

The train begins to move. It crosses the bridge to Irun and she makes out the shape of a small island floating calm as a boat. Beneath the nail of her left index finger there is a tattoo of purple blood, a hood-shaped mark which does not signify martyrdom. It is merely a blemish which will fade soon.

Bilbao

Bilbao is a kaleidoscope before a tired woman's eyes.

The bus which rattles and groans to that destination is rusted red and yellow. Her fellow passengers lack even banal touches of exoticism – there are no peasants carrying caged fowl or sad-eyed teenage runaways – so to pass the time and to keep herself awake, Gisèle tries to analyse them using the categories from August Sander's *Face of our time*. She's always admired the portraits in Sander's book, although she finds the seven categories he used to describe the people of the German nation somewhat reductive. Where would Sander place the thin-faced girl wearing a patterned headscarf gazing out the window into darkness? Well, under Woman naturally, just as he would have probably put the man wearing the stiff-collared black suit in Classes and Professions and the couple opposite, who are laden with produce and look as though they might operate a small tavern, in the City. But perhaps the man in the dark suit is actually a successful landscape painter; therefore he should be placed in the Artists. Why is there one category for Woman and six for everyone else? If the young woman were actually a prostitute, would this justify her inclusion in Classes and Professions?

Gisèle stops her fruitless analysis. The National Socialists smashed up the photographic plates of Sander's book and burnt the existing copies; she would rather sleep than think about it.

The driver's voice jolts her awake just before midnight. If the train from San Sebastian hadn't broken down, thus necessitating this later bus, she would have arrived two hours ago and not have to be thinking about how to reach the hotel room.

Gisèle stumbles off the bus, aware of an intermittent line of pain between her eyes and an aching lassitude in her limbs. She takes her case from the luggage hold and looks around. She has the address written down but perhaps she should not bother trying to find it and take her chances at the nearest fleapit.

She is still standing, watching a horse-drawn cart pass along the street when the bus driver approaches and stands so close she can see the blackheads clustering on the slope of his left cheek. Inadvertently, she warns him away in French; then, glad that the word is the same in both languages, asks 'Taxi?' and shows him the slip of paper with the printed address.

He points through the darkness and makes no move to help her with the suitcase.

The taxi is older than the bus. She shows the man inside the slip of paper. He grunts and drives through the snarled skein of streets which she feels closing around her like a net. She hasn't eaten anything since the cheese roll on the train from Toulouse but the thought of food produces a nauseous surge in her gut. The dirt accumulated over days of travelling now feels part of her, like a skin. She longs to wash off the identity of Veronique Baudin, to leave her lying, limp as a shroud, folded neatly next to a long white porcelain tub. She hopes that the pension arranged for her stay (yet another example of Victoria's long and generous reach) has a bath.

Her destination turns out to be one street back from the river. Gisèle smells the dankness of tidal evaporation and makes out the shapes of small moored watercraft. A solitary streetlight lights a row of double-storied stucco houses coloured mint, cadmium and a dusty chalk blue. She hammers on the door then hammers again until a yellow pane of light forms on the second floor while the driver waits, arms folded, glowering, slouched against the bonnet of his vehicle.

The woman who eventually answers is middle-aged, dressed in black, surely a close cousin of all those who rule the lives of apartment dwellers in France with a control born of unending scrutiny. Now she scrutinises Gisèle and, by the expression on her face, the opinion formed is not favourable.

'Senora Ocampo…'

Regardless of her opinion, Victoria's name unlocks the treasure chest: pesetas are produced; the driver disappears. The concierge gives some more of these, a small amount, to Gisèle who knows that the woman will have also lined her own pockets. She is probably in the early years of middle age but the black clothes give the appearance of a life largely gone. She jerks her head, unspeaking, in the direction of the stairs.

Sweat beads Gisèle's forehead as she hauls up the case. There is a fractured dazzle behind her eyes; she has to wait for these spasms of light to subside before she can take in the yellow-painted walls and the bed with fresh sheets, a pile of pillows and a striped linen counterpane. Scarlet flowers in an earthenware jug momentarily raise a throb of pain from her eyes but there is the other jug on the small table next to the bed and Gisèle stumbles to this oasis, moaning softly. She pours herself a glass of water then pitches to the bed.

She drinks one glass then another. She rummages in the suitcase, cursing, searching and, yes, there are some aspirin packed, along with other medicinal supplies, by Mademoiselle Devereaux. Gisèle blesses that industrious virgin while she swallows the tablets and wishes the ringing in her ears would stop. The machines on which she has travelled for so long seem to have unleashed an echoing symmetry her brain can't turn off. Nevertheless, eventually, she sleeps.

Sometime during the night, she wakes, sweating and crying out in the darkness. She fumbles for the glass, drinks, lets it fall to the floor and sleeps again.

Next morning, her headache is worse and her cheeks are unnaturally flushed, although the ringing in her ears has stopped. Her room has shutters which open onto a small balcony so she pushes them open and stands surveying the city. To the west, she sees the distant sweep of the Nervion River, widening as it becomes an estuary that enters the Bay of Biscay. Across the river there is the sprawl of the port stretching for miles, the industrial jumble of steelyards and shipyards, cleaved and spliced to the east by railway lines. She can make out the craters where German bombs landed five years ago. On this side of the river, to the east, are houses and a church's Gothic spire.

There is a loud knocking on the door. The concierge has brought breakfast but Gisèle refuses food and instead runs water in the bath at the end of the corridor. She steps naked through clouds of steam and lies in a long white porcelain tub, one arm thrown limply over its edge. There are dainty soaps scented with rose and lavender and something English and green. She is boneless, nerveless, etiolated.

She understands suddenly that resistance can become a chore, that the strongest will can be eroded, so that surrender is chosen and annihilation beckons voluptuously. It would be so easy to sink below the surface, like a heartsick girl surrounded by flowers and river reeds or a pock-marked revolutionary, breast bared to the assassin's knife or a mad genius weighting her cardigan pockets with stones.

Gisèle realises that she must walk or sink. She heaves herself up and almost falls. In the mirror, she glimpses the ribs ridging the plain of her body; it is hard to believe that Adrienne once adored this skin and these limbs with her lips and hands.

She puts on her one clean dress, an unbecoming black gridded with white. Mercifully, overnight, her menstruation has ceased; it will do that these days, stop abruptly. For a moment, she contemplates breaking off one of the poppies in the vase and wearing it in her belt but realises that in this country, red is now a bad colour choice.

She moves down the stairs as quietly as she can in order to avoid the concierge but the woman skewers her movements with all-seeing eyes.

Outside, the air is clammy. Gisèle has read somewhere that this place is prone to fog; as she walks through the streets, parallel to the river, she tries to remember street names, to orient herself in a way that will facilitate a safe return, but the signs in the unfamiliar language blur. She comes to a strip of parkland then crosses a narrow footbridge which takes her over a railway line and into the Calle de Buenos Aires. She knows she should stick to the main thoroughfares but, as always, she is lured by the unknown and forsakes the promise of safety to move into back streets and side alleys. After a few noisy blocks, the port is behind her.

She stops outside a café where groups of men sit at tables. Surreptitiously, she examines the patrons, notes that they are mainly shabby and still young. One is missing his left leg below the knee, another wears a patch over his right eye. They must have been on the same side but which side was that? She is reminded of the veterans she used to see in Berlin as a teenager. Their faces had so often worn the same expression she sees through the window now, closed and bitter. If she had the Leica with her, she would risk documenting their hostility even though she knows that photographers have been killed for less.

Not everyone is marked by the stigmata of war. A young man on a building site winks at her as she passes. She smells the maleness of his sweat, sees a ripples of muscle beneath thin cloth; if she were not feeling so faint, she would be aroused. She wonders how he remembers that time, whether there were people in his family who died.

It is not just the human body which carries scars. Buildings can rise again from rubble but memories are not so easily erased. Old hatreds can linger for generations, seeping subterranean poison, hidden behind rising shields of concrete and glass.

She crosses a park and at the intersection of Alameda and Poza, a group of children approach, shepherded by a nun in black. The children walk in neatly aligned couples and seem, to Gisèle's inexperienced eyes, to range in age from six to ten.

They are thin and quiet; only one boy, wearing a shirt the sleeves of which reach past his wrists, seems lively, laughing and trying to break away from his partner. As they pass Gisèle, the nun grabs the child's ear. *'Tu padre era un criminal! Tu madre era una puta!'* she hisses.

Gisèle utters a small exclamation; flat brown eyes stare back at her from beneath the coif. The child's eyes are tear-filled although he doesn't utter a sound. He is no doubt learning that no one hears. Perhaps he has stopped crying at night, in the bed of the orphanage which is home. Gisèle wants to intervene, to upbraid the woman. Pointless, if not dangerous: the nun has God and the state on her side in her care of these children of the Republic.

She and her charges are quickly lost in the throng of passing pedestrians. All Gisèle can do is renew her vow to remain a stony bed of rock, the waterhole in the desert which dries to sand. If she could find a doctor willing to do it, she would have herself spayed.

She must rest. The sun is now quite hot and has dispersed the dampness in the air. Gisèle changes course, walks towards a strand of shops which advertise themselves in blonde wood, bright paint and chrome. Gisèle enters one, takes a seat on a stool at the window and orders a glass of wine. Two women sitting at a nearby table, well-dressed and hair sleekly groomed, glance at her disparagingly. One says something and the other, who is pregnant, laughs. Laugh on, you bitches, Gisèle thinks grimly, history will rebound on you tenfold although, even as she forms the words, she knows they are histrionic and almost certainly destined to be false. She knows that it is pointless to cogitate on what might have been but she can't help it: if the countries which now call themselves the Allies had intervened on the Republican side, if American and British corporations hadn't given money to Franco, then it is just possible that she would not be sitting here, that the present cataclysm might have been avoided. If, if, if...

Two men, obviously from the professional class, join the women and Gisèle is suddenly aware that she is the only female sitting on her own. She knows that in fascist Spain, as in Hitler's Germany, female autonomy is discouraged and actively legislated against. Women are to be breeders, first and foremost, although in Spain they have the doubtful refuge of the convent. Gisèle sips her wine, which is dry, slightly sparkling and very good. She picks at the dish of olives provided and is tempted to ask for another glass but the stare she receives from the man behind the counter tells her it is politic to leave.

She should at least have drunk a glass of water, she realises, as she walks on. The sun and the wine swell her tongue but public fountains elude her, her vision blurs and the ache in her legs has become pain. She turns down one narrow side street which at least offers some shade then enters the alley which runs off that because she thinks she can hear the glistening

drip

drip

drip

of silver…

The alley becomes a cul-de-sac ending in a fringe of dusty elms and, between two of them, shallow steps descend to a courtyard, part of which is slimy with moss. A thread of water falls from a pipe. Across the courtyard is a high wall into which is set a heavy arched gate.

Gisèle puts her face under the pipe then, because its intermittent leak is not enough for her thirst, she kneels at the pool which has formed beneath it. She bathes her face and begins to drink until she is lifted roughly to her feet.

Gisèle turns, ready to flail at this assailant but she sees that she has nothing to fear: the face before her is melancholy with hooded eyes which carry no threat of violence. In her imperfect grasp of Spanish, he seems to be warning her about some threat of disease. Perhaps he sees the branching flames of illness consuming her body because he then suggests a doctor.

'No, no doctor! He'll make me stay in this country and I'll die here! No doctor!' Gisèle shouts, struggling out of his grasp, then, because she is raving, '*How I loathe all professions…!*'

'*…masters and workers, you are all vile peasants,*' he finishes with her, gently, speaking French. 'So, no doctor. But you definitely need assistance.'

Gisèle suddenly totters. She clutches at him. He swings open the barred gate and ushers her behind it. For a moment, they are both becalmed in Rimbaud's drunken boat, speaking his language, rocking gently on an ocean of calamity. He unlocks the door and they enter a cavern where a black and white cat snarls then scurries and a saffron finch sings from a cage. There is a smell, dusty and familiar, evoking memories of hard-backed chairs and monastic silence.

'I will return soon.'

He disappears in the direction of the cat and Gisèle wonders uneasily about his destination and his intent but gradually her eyes adjust to the darkness. She understands the smell of must and decay when she sees the shelves of books which fill the room. Sounds emanate behind her, the clink of a spoon, the smell of smoke: something is being heated on a wood stove. Eventually he returns and hands her a cup of bitter green. Gisèle drinks. It has been flavoured with honey but that cannot entirely disguise the astringent taste of young sap rising through trees in springtime.

For the first time, she takes in her rescuer. He is reaching the outpost of middle age, with the skin of someone who refuses sunlight. She notices as he moves around his library that there's a hitch to his walk, barely bad enough to be called a limp.

He sees her looking. 'There were some problems I needed to escape in 1915 so I joined the Legion. The limp is a souvenir. It's why I can speak your language.'

'It's not my language,' Gisèle says, then wonders if she will ever be able to call any language hers again. Not German; not now, when the verb 'spritzen', once used to refer to the bubbles in red wine, has come to describe the spurting of Jewish blood; but not French, not yet, and not English. Perhaps Spanish will become her language. She turns towards him and proffers the cup, which he refills.

He also brings a few thin slices of dark bread. 'Eat a little.'

Gisèle nibbles, fighting back a gust of nausea. 'So you survived the war, then there was the next one…'

'I played no part in that, mademoiselle. I kept my peace. What I saw with the Legion turned me against all wars.' He regards her for a moment. 'There is only art. Only literature.'

Gisèle is tempted to obscenity, to tell him that his sentiment is rubbish, garbage, *merde*, but she holds her tongue. The tea has revived her; her body has pushed the illness into temporary retreat. She sees, from the titles which she is able to decipher, that the books on the shelves are muck, disposable trash, just like *The lives of the saints*, left on the seat of the railway carriage at Hendaye. There are some of the Maigret novels which Walter Benjamin loved and other potboilers she saw him reading, in Berlin, in Frankfurt, in Paris, over the years. She recognises a title by Mary Renault, about a married doctor who has an affair with a younger woman. Gisèle has read it, during her early days in France, and thought it merely a superior type of romance novel, fit only for housewives.

'You put your faith in popular fiction?' Despite her best intentions, she cannot keep the sneer out of her voice.

He smiles, seemingly not offended. 'There are worse things to live by, much worse. Escapism is not necessarily harmful.'

'Not true, when it keeps the escapee from engaging with the problems of the world.'

He regards her silently then smiles as though she has just passed an exam in a difficult subject. 'Follow me.'

He moves a low table beneath with is an ancient threadbare mat and pulls up a trapdoor. The ladder down is steep; Gisèle sways, grips the sides, descends. A single yellowish bulb burns. Her heart resumes it normal rhythm in the same length of time it takes her eyes to adjust to the umber glow.

She walks slowly between the shelves touching leather-bound spines, greeting some as old friends, others as worthy adversaries. For some time, she is bewildered, lost in this forest of words, then she understands: he's selling off libraries assembled in Vienna, Berlin, Prague; in Budapest and in Paris. Some of these books are on the Index, illegal in a re-Catholicised Spain. In Germany, books were burnt; here they are merely caged furtively in darkness at the bottom of stone steps. Here are the books, unloved and unread, scholarship about language, science and philosophy which are now just words buried beneath the scum of history.

Amazingly, there is a copy, the gold letters on the cover gleaming, of Walter Benjamin's *The origins of German tragic drama*, published in 1928. Gisèle leaves it alone. She knows, rationally, that it carries no contagion, that touching it will not occasion bad luck; even so, she leaves it alone.

Nearby is a section of books in Hebrew. She sees a title by Walter's Zionist friend Gershon Scholem,

She wonders if the bookseller can understand that language – she can't – but before she can ask he says, 'I can read that, just a little. We were a family who survived the flames. We converted rather than be burnt, so everything we had was driven underground.'

And so to this cellar, Gisèle thinks. She glimpses a long struggle, fragmentation, a precious vessel dropped, shattered, put back together. Threads of an old shawl painstakingly pulled together and patched, hidden away for so long that its function was almost forgotten. But always, something held…

On a bench at the back of the room she finds a tray of dusty postcards, hand-coloured photographs showing scenes of Bilbao before the Civil War. There are views across the river, with all the bridges intact; palm trees in a public garden and an imposing neo-Baroque theatre. Gisèle takes several. For some reason, these wan pastel shades remind her of Atget's photographs of nineteenth-century Parisian streets and shopfronts. They produce the same feeling of abandonment in the viewer, nostalgia which crosses over into desolation. She remembers Adrienne told her once that the American Berenice Abbott bought up many of Atget's plate-glass negatives and took them with her when she left Paris in 1929. Gisèle never met Abbott but has seen her portrait of Sylvia dressed in a shiny black raincoat. Gisèle laughs. On some people, such a garment could have looked rather erotic, even kinky. On Sylvia, it just looked like something to keep the weather out.

Gisèle is just about to say that she would rather be upstairs, for the dust is making her nose run and eyes sting when she sees a book she has heard about but never read, by a young woman who was once acclaimed, a best-seller in Weimar.

Gisèle picks it up. It's small, as light as a handful of dried grass, the pages already browning although it was published only five years ago, in Holland.

She opens the book at random and reads, 'The roofs that you see are not built for you. The bread that you smell is not baked for you. And the language that you hear is not spoken for you.'

The flood, which Gisèle has been containing for so long, breaks suddenly. The estuary of tears within her, for the dead and the maimed, spills over and she weeps. She weeps. She weeps. She weeps.

Elsa's parents were not able to view their daughter's body; the coffin lid had been nailed down.

She weeps for Elsa, for the dead blonde girl she saw one winter morning, pulled from the Seine, for Walter Benjamin hauling himself through the mountains, willing his damaged heart to endure. She weeps for the loss, the shame, for everything which is gone.

Somewhere, in all this, she is aware of being helped to sit in a commodious leather chair. Cloth is draped over her…

'Happy birthday, Zelli.' Her father hands her the small rectangular box wrapped in shiny blue paper.

She's careful with the paper, not wanting to appear childish in her eagerness on this, her sixteenth birthday. Nevertheless, she squeals with delight as she sees the name on the box, because the Leica is exactly what she wants…

When the bookseller shakes her awake, Gisèle knows that she has been crying out.

'You must leave now,' he says without preamble. 'It will be dark soon and it's not safe for you to be on the streets after night fall.'

He hands her a small paper bag which crackles faintly when Gisèle takes it: she understands that it is more of what he brewed for her before.

She picks up the book and the postcards then returns the book to its shelf. She knows that she is depriving him of income but she cannot afford to be caught with a book which was openly critical of Hitler's regime. He notices what she does but makes no comment. He is a trader in risk who understands the risks taken by those who trade with him.

Shakily, Gisèle climbs the ladder then waits until he emerges behind her and drops the trapdoor. As she hands over the money, she wants to thank him for his mercy but all she can do is ask him for the toilet, which turns out to be hole in the ground above a stinking pit in the yard at the back of the shop.

'I don't know how to get back…'

'Where are you staying?'

When she returns from the yard, he hands her a map drawn in spidery black ink.

'It's not so far but go quickly.' He escorts her to the gate.

The light is still bright but has a richer, deeper tint, gold which will soon shade to dusk. Small eddies of dust rise from the courtyard, whipped up by the wind.

'Go quickly,' he tells her, locking the gate. 'There's a storm coming.'

'And we have to call this storm progress,' mutters Gisèle, as she sets off. Her face feels tight, mask-like, from dried tears but also slightly cooler. She hurries along the alley with its piles of garbage and shadows which throw Frankenstein shapes, turns into the side street where a man emerging from a doorway puts his hand on his crotch and calls. Gisèle runs, she stumbles on the cobbles, conscious of how weak she is but makes it down the street back to the main thoroughfare. The shops, which have been shut during the heat of the afternoon, are reopening but café proprietors are taking in tables and chairs from outside as the wind gathers strength.

When Gisèle stops, gasping, and examines the map she sees that she has not actually travelled very far, that she has moved in a rough circle, and that the pension can be reached by walking a little further then crossing a bridge. Nothing occurs to endanger her; even so, she does not feel safe until she crosses that bridge.

Later, as she sits sipping a cup of the bookseller's bitter brew in the pension, she tries to remember what happened to the novel's young author and seems to recall that she committed suicide, another casualty of the times. *Not me*, thinks Gisèle. Whatever happens: they can beat me, torture me, kill me but they are going to have to take that trouble. I will not sacrifice myself. Not me. In memory of Walter, of Virginia, of poor anguished Irmgard Keun, I will go on, until I cannot any longer…

Abruptly she rushes to the sink and vomits greenish liquid and brown slime. The concierge, coming into the room to tell her that the taxi has arrived, begins a string of Spanish of which Gisèle catches only *doctor en Medicina*…

'No, no doctor! If you call a doctor, I'll die here!' she shouts in French. 'I'm not going to die! Not me!'

The woman throws up her hands and retreats.

Not me. *Not* me. The words become an iron spike to which she is chained while the wind buffets her into the taxi. The spike is driven between her eyes to form a red-hot pit as the suburbs pass and the black water of the river meets the tidal swell of the Bay of Biscay.

Not me. Not me. Gisèle holds on, although the spike impales her vision. The boat towers above her, quivers in a tunnel of pain, dissolves then reappears, trapped, unmoving, by a net of stars. She can't be sure that it's real. Not until she feels the deck beneath her feet, sees the steady metallic churn of water behind, and knows that this vessel, pitching and rearing, has reached open sea, does she let go.

'Not me!'

The world glitters like a handful of silver; the light abrades her eyes, then she falls down blindly into darkness.

Black/silver/white

Blackness…

…pierced by brilliant shades of light then…

…blackness…

…she must be back at the table five years old in a white dress looking at the light from the chandelier…

Blackness…

…there is a long cold plunge through black water…

…before she rises from a bleak river grave; sodden white flesh pulled from the river, black clothes embedded with black leaves and black dirt. The photographer aims a camera, there is a bursting flash of white, a corpse embalmed as image…

…a white face bends over her, tilts from side to side, slides from view…

…there are the blank eyes in rows of marble statues, a hand raised in salute against a glittering sky…

…the face returns, attached to a white body and wielding a silver spear. There is a sliver of pain which spreads fire down her arm and…

…leaping white streaks of flame, her father wearing a black suit holding her mother in a white dress while she weeps, moaning softly, 'Willi, Theo.' There is candlelight through glass, silver cutlery and white damask, Maria carrying the silver tureen to table…

…the face…

…in a white room with a black coffin and a voice, well modulated, she knows it is usually gentle and kind but now it snaps with urgency: 'Zelli, Zelli, it's time to leave, there's a storm coming…'

…and somewhere, always, a wind howls…

She wakes in a white room where the light gleams coldly off chrome. Sun coming through a window impales her with brightness. She winces, cries out at its ferocity, is aware of the face bending over her, then she sleeps again.

When she wakes next time, the window is black. She glimpses the moon and stars, sees the obsidian ocean and the roil of black water…

…a man wearing a white coat comes into the room. Fluorescent light glitters off the small round glasses he wears. He smiles. 'So, at last you have returned to us.' He speaks English but Gisèle sees that he is not English; something about his bearing reminds her of her father, the Prussian posture affected even by civilians. His smile scarcely renders his face less serious. 'We thought we might lose you…'

'How long have I been away?'

'This is the seventh day.'

Gisèle, who feels as disoriented as a time traveller returning from another planet, remembers her manners. 'I'm so sorry…'

'It's my job.' He smiles again. A gleam of mischief warms his face and Gisèle sees the young man, a prankster and lover of jokes, 'but you did keep telling the nurse you were the angel of history and she didn't know quite what to make of that.'

Gisèle tries to laugh but the sound is water drying in a rusty pipe.

'You've had influenza. Normally, it wouldn't have been so serious but you were malnourished, very run-down physically, which meant that your immune system buckled and almost broke. I don't know how you were infected…'

'It was the breath of a fallen angel,' Gisèle tells him before she drifts to the restful country of oblivion, where there are no dreams, just a continuous white sea of sleep.

The following day, she is deemed well enough to sit swaddled on the deck for a short time. The boat cuts the ocean, oyster-coloured stippled with pale blue, reflecting vapours of cloud. She sits wrapped in a blanket, watching droplets of water slide down the sides of a glass as though they contained the world. Africa has passed like a mirage. (It remains a place of imagination, somewhere she never visits.) They have entered the tropics; long-tailed birds perform acrobatics in the warm air.

Fragments of her delirium return, her minds shimmers, the past feels transparent, porous: she remembers photographing the drowned girl pulled from the Seine, water running in rivulets from rat tails of blonde hair. At the time she had thought, 'Elsa', with only the hair showing; however, the face, eventually turned for the camera's eye, was blunted-featured, unintelligent-looking, nothing like the one she had loved.

It had been Roger Caillois who had told her a newspaper editor wanted a photograph of that particular incident; that was the beginning, the first photo she had sold in Paris, not long before she met Adrienne.

The first day she met Adrienne, they walked in the Luxembourg Gardens, had stood looking at the twin rows of marble statues: there was Marguerite d'Anjou, clasping her doomed son, Edward VII, killed during the War of the Roses in 1371.

'She was an exile, like you, even though she was a queen,' Adrienne had said. She gazed ironically at the frozen drapes of cloth crusted with lichen, the eyes staring sightlessly through history: 'Indeed we are fortunate, mademoiselle. Always we have been either royalty or saints.'

'A little different, these days, surely?'

'A little.'

There had been a high wind, ozone in the air which charged their blood. Gisèle had wanted to photograph this living flesh and blood woman as a contrast to all this bland stone but when she raised the Leica, Adrienne, perceiving her intent, had dodged with surprising speed behind Louise of Savoy. A chase had ensued, past Jeanne of Navarre and Mary, Queen of Scots, Genevieve, patron saint of Paris and Matilda, wife of William the Conqueror.

At Saint Berthe de Laen, mother of Charlemagne, Gisèle had admitted defeat. 'All right, then. Have it your own way.' She replaced the lens cap and handed the camera to Adrienne. 'If I can't photograph you, then you must photograph me.'

'I can –'

'Yes you can. Sometimes it really is as easy as pressing the shutter.' Gisèle lit a cigarette.

Momentarily the sun emerged, vanquishing the encroaching clouds, and she had turned her face towards it, raising her right hand, palm valiant, fingers spread. This was the photograph Adrienne had made, the moment at which, she later told Gisèle, she fell in love.

Sunlight reflecting off a window behind Gisèle creates a burst of light which calls up another memory, something from so long ago it sleeps beneath layers of experience, suppressed by the strata of years. There is something primal here, which might illuminate self-knowledge: her mind scrabbles, tries to claim it but it slips beyond reach.

Gisèle gives up. Sometimes the lines are too faintly etched, the script distorted, unintelligible. She sips from the glass of water, disembodied, insubstantial, unable to contemplate food. She feels distant gratitude to the doctor and the petite, dark-haired nurse who changes her sheets and brings her tablets.

The doctor has a story but she does not want to learn it: all she knows is that she has survived while others have perished.

Over three days, colour returns to her world, an edging of dark brown, a seep of beige, sliding amber beads set in silver which herald a sickle-shaped red hat perched above a matching suit, green-patterned tablecloths in the breakfast room, the ocean cerulean beneath the sun. She avoids conversations, negotiates the overtures of a friendly American who is on a mission to buy beef from the Argentines.

He is the one who tells her about the tremendous storm endured on the way across before commiserating her on her illness and taking her hand. 'I know BA quite well. When I'm done doing business, I could show you the sights.'

Gisèle gently retracts. 'My fiancée was killed at Dunkerque. I'm on my way to take the veil with an order of the Sacred Heart.'

As tugs drag the boat up the Rio de la Plata, the River of Silver, to the city the Spaniards named for the Virgin who preserved them from shipwreck and storm, Gisèle stands at the ship's railing, chaste as a saint, watching the spray of water. People push past, intent on their own business. A polyglot gabble surrounds her: Spanish; another language, similar, but with more open vowel sounds which she assumes is Portuguese. There is French, English, also the German dialect spoken in northern Austria, others she can't identify. 'You won't forget to write now, will you?' and 'Your company has made such a difference on this voyage.'

Forgotten by the time they're down the gangway, thinks Gisèle, and pays no further attention. Shipboard relationships must be like most friendships formed when travelling, transient, made in the knowledge that there is no obligation to continue once journey's end is reached.

She watches as the boat is drawn alongside the wharf and the gangway lowered. She has reached the New World but she feels no relief or joy, only a weary kind of calm. Standing at the railing, she is transparent, pure as a square of white linen, waiting for time to write itself upon her. Events before this voyage seem distant, elusive as the shadow of a bird glimpsed through gauze curtains.

Part Three

Buenos Aires

This hothouse, the city

Gisèle stands on the dock, suddenly a creature of land, her muscles liquefying, blinking in the light. The batter of language intensifies and she sways, dizzy from the swirl of sound. Always it seems that she has to begin again: another country, a new tongue. She is forever a transplant in alien soil.

With an effort, she steadies herself, wishes for water; then she follows the trail of people moving to the U-shaped complex of buildings at the end of the dock where fans whir overhead and two men sit behind a desk on a raised dais. Gisèle sees that they are both pot-bellied and greasy-haired, like standard South Americans in a Hollywood B-grade film: mentally she names them Larger Belly and Smaller Belly. A thin man in a long black coat manifestly unsuited to the warm humid day hands over money to them which makes Gisèle uneasily aware that she has very little left. Will the men behind the desk expect the same from her and, if so, has Victoria taken care of it? Above the men a row of clocks show the time for various cities in the world. Twenty metres behind them is the door through which passengers pass on their way out; next to the door a small window shows some of the blurred faces of those who wait in Argentina.

The line crawls forward. The clock showing Argentine time reads 10.20. Gisèle wishes she had something to read or something to eat: her appetite has suddenly returned with a vengeance.

When the clock reads 11.37, she reaches the head of the line and presents her passport with the other papers required.

Larger Belly examines the passport closely, turns it over slowly in his hands then speaks to his colleague, who sniggers. They both look Gisèle over as though they are examining meat on the hoof.

My name is Veronique Baudin.

There is more sniggering, then Larger Belly rises from the desk and walks away. Smaller Belly barks at her in Spanish and gestures to a series of cubicles which line one side of the room.

A saying of Sylvia Beach's, one of the many maxims that buzzing little American woman possessed, rings in Gisèle's ears: 'Don't fall at the last hurdle.' (She heard Sylvia say this over the phone to Ernest Hemingway, in 1939, when Hemingway was having trouble with the final chapters of *For Whom the Bell Tolls.*) She can't believe she's come all this way, only to be refused entry at the portal to freedom. The floor suddenly dips and spins. She sits down on the chair provided and tries to think although the stuffiness created by the press of people in this space has turned her brain to fuzz. She must, somehow, contact Victoria.

This building is a crate, a prison, from which she may never escape; then a voice reaches her, familiar, but unheard for such a long time she can't quite believe in it. Gisèle rises and looks over the top of the cubicle.

The man to whom the voice belongs seems to sense her presence and turns, smiling. He beckons her across then kisses her on both cheeks. 'It seems my fate to be your welcoming committee, my dear escapee.'

Gisèle breaks into a babble, a waterfall of words, she can't help it, the sounds crescendos, for here is Roger Caillois, debonair and ambiguous, not much changed from when she last saw him in Paris in 1939, about to leave for his lecture tour of South America. World events have stranded him in Argentina but he seems none the worse.

'There seems to be a problem but I don't know what it is…'

He makes a silencing motion. 'Please leave this to me.' He addresses the officials in Spanish.

Gisèle can't understand what they are saying but she catches the word puta and is astounded. Do these men really think she is a whore? It's not as though she is standing here in a red dress with an overpainted face; then she remembers the prostitute she photographed in Frankfurt in 1929. There had been nothing exotic or flamboyant about that woman: she had just been ground down by poverty and was probably desperate to feed her children. Had it been right to make a study of someone's hopelessness? Gisèle had been twenty-one then and so determined to learn her craft she hadn't thought about any deeper ethical issues.

In front of her, Roger Caillois shouts, throws his hands in the air, gestures towards Gisèle and speaks to the men once more who burst into laughter. One claps Roger Caillois on the shoulder and indicates the door at the end of the building. He picks up her suitcase and, placing his free hand beneath her elbow, steers Gisèle towards it.

'What did you say to them?'

'It's best you don't know. It is all taken care of. I am sorry I had to denigrate you – but whatever possessed you to put down "artist" on your passport?'

'That was nothing to do with me. It was probably Adrienne's idea...'

'Well, Adrienne should have known better. It would have been wiser to have you listed as a hairdresser or a nurse.'

'I have a loathing of needles and the sight of blood makes me sick...'

'Then I advise you, when you get another passport, to list your occupation as photographer. "Artist" makes men here think that you are at best an artist's model, at worst, an artist of the streets.' He smiles, warningly. 'Attitudes are different here. It's almost unheard of for a woman to have a career – and it marks her as a failure, not a real woman.' He holds the door open. 'Now, shall we forget this sorry incident and proceed?'

As she passes through, the light assaults Gisèle. Its brightness renders much of her training obsolete; here is another language she will have to learn. She is so dazed by the sun that she steps off the kerb without looking and it is only Roger Caillois's vigilance which saves her from being run down.

'Gisèle! Let us try to get to the car without any more drama!'

The car is large and English, not something an expatriate intellectual could afford. He opens the door then takes his place beside her and steers expertly into the traffic coursing by the docks. Gisèle smiles.

'What amuses you?' he asks as they cross a railway line.

'I can't help contrasting this to my arrival in Paris in 1933. It was raining, there was no one to meet me and, besides my papers, I had only a toothbrush.'

Roger Caillois laughs. 'Even an exile can go up in the world, eh?' He slows to allow a group of pedestrians disembarking from a tram to cross the street then continues. 'Madame Victoria telegraphed the ship when you were en route. She knows that you have been very ill, so she has opened the house at Palermo Chico for a month. She thinks that this is a better place for you to recuperate and to get to know the city, given that you will be with us for some time. Later, perhaps...' he swings the car briskly northwest, through a busy intersection, '...you might like to stay at the house at San Isidro, which is where she usually is, and where I usually am.'

Gisèle does not respond, just lights a cigarette and inhales deeply. The idea of being taken care of, being ministered to, is strange but for the moment she relaxes into it, feeling embraced. She sinks back against the car's beige leather seat and watches the city slide by, a grid of wide white streets on which modern office blocks stand next to tiered colonial buildings, embellished with balustrades and arches. She knows that this city is called the Paris of South America so, at first, she looks for similarities.

She realises that, apart from an architectural skin, these are few. This city is a hothouse, its sensuality flamboyant, less contained than French culture. On balconies and in parks she sees plants with broad flat leaves and flowers as big as plates. The streets are crowded, the faces on them as diverse as the languages she has heard spoken. This is a transplanted culture, many nationalities grafted to a vast, scarcely trammelled landscape. There are northern Europeans, southern Europeans, a few blacks. Gisèle even spots a pair of Hassidic Jews deep in conversation.

'They are probably recent arrivals,' Roger Caillois tells her. 'There are many refugees here.'

As the car passes a small park, she sees a cluster of people with flat, Asiatic-style faces, wearing capes and calls his attention to them. 'Are they Indians, natives?'

He regards them briefly and dismissively. 'There are not many of them left. They will die out soon.' He follows her gaze further along the street.

Gisèle is watching a young woman with wavy lustrous dark hair. She wears a black skirt which follows the curve of her hips, has shapely calves curved into black stockings.

'Nice, huh?'

They laugh together then drive on past the Casa Rosada, office of the Argentine president. Gisèle asks the question all tourists ask, about the rose-pink stone which gave the group of buildings its name.

'Legend has it that the colour was created to symbolise reconciliation between the two major parties of the time: one was identified by red, the other by white. Of course, if that was the aim, then an examination of Argentine politics shows that it's been a dismal failure. President Ortiz won't last much longer. He's sick and, unlike you, he will not recover. Perhaps, soon, there will be a chance for this era of corruption to end and for things to change for the better. But the British still have the government in their pockets so…' He breaks off, smiling slightly.

'Who are the contenders for power?'

'Ramon Castillo has been effectively running things for several years now and will in all likelihood assume formal office soon. There's the army, of course – there's always the army, here. Some people speak of an officer, Juan Carlos Perón, but he is not to be taken seriously, just a buffoon in a uniform.'

'I recall people in Europe saying much the same thing about another buffoon, not long out of uniform: "not to be taken seriously",' replies Gisèle drily.

Roger Caillois laughs sardonically then lapses into silence. Gisèle regards his profile. She has noted the slightly possessive manner in which he referred to Victoria earlier. If he is hoping that their affair will end in marriage, then he can forget that: Adrienne has told her enough for Gisèle to know that Victoria will never enter into that state again.

'When she was young, she made a disastrous marriage, undertaken to escape the stifling proprieties of her parental home, from which the laws in Catholic Argentina would not release her. For all her elegance, wealth and intelligence, Victoria had the status of a chained dog in her husband's house.'

Adrienne had told her this, not long after Gisèle's own marriage, as they lounged together in Adrienne's apartment, early one morning. Gisèle had just found out that she needed Pierre Blum's signature in order to obtain her own passport. Gisèle had exploded angrily; Adrienne had sympathised but then jokily told her that at least she would be able to divorce her husband without too much trouble. That was why she had mentioned Victoria's past predicament.

Adrienne had continued, as she idly stroked the skin at the opening of Gisèle's robe. 'For all her servants and couture, Victoria is strong. She must have learned strength when she battled for a legal separation; endurance during its long years, until her husband's death made it unnecessary; discretion, as she maintained a relationship with a married man. But those qualities, which have gone into making her such a successful editor as well as the friend and confidante of many writers, have come at a price.'

The car enters a street lined with shade trees. The gardens of the large houses have deep lawns ornamented by baroque swells of vegetation, succulent crimsons, purples and greens which look slightly predatory in their abundance. They turn into a wide driveway gravelled with white stone and draw up before a large white house, its many balconies ornamented with black wrought iron.

A man with skin the colour of weak coffee emerges to take Gisèle's case. Roger Caillois speaks to him in Spanish, indicating the car. Gisèle emerges slowly, her legs have cramped then stands looking about her just as an exquisitely groomed woman wearing a powder-blue Chanel suit walks from the house. In one hand, she holds a silk scarf coloured yellow, scarlet and viridian, in the other a bunch of orchids.

'Here is a shawl for my Veronique,' the woman greets her, in French. She mimes wiping her face then laughs while the silk streams in the breeze like a pennant of victory. This is Victoria Ocampo, a woman given to gestures of extravagant generosity, who once sent poor dead Virginia Woolf a box of butterflies, their brilliant wings perfectly impaled behind glass.

'Gisèle!' Victoria embraces her and arranges the scarf. 'Gisèle! Welcome!' Then, looking at her seriously, 'I'm so glad you're here. I did wonder if I would see you again, after I heard how ill you were.'

'It was just some flu,' Gisèle replies. She still feels like a tourist in her own body but here is Victoria, naming her, birthing her into the New World.

And in response, Gisèle lets fly with another glissando of sound: impressions, questions and a babbled commentary which is also a greeting slide over one another, punctuated by a brief thunderstorm which erupts from nowhere. All three race for the house, lashed by warm rain.

Inside, Victoria holds up her hands in laughing protest then disappears briefly; when she returns she's holding a glossily wrapped package. 'This is for you.'

'I'm sorry,' Gisèle says, as she struggles with the paper. 'It's been so long since I could talk to people freely and I want to learn all about this new place.'

'You could live here a lifetime and still not understand it,' Victoria replies. 'We who are born here don't understand it, and because of that, we don't understand ourselves.' Her gaze becomes pensive, almost melancholy.

She turns her face toward the beds of brightly coloured flowers visible through the windows, beyond which rise the glass walls of a hothouse. The light, filtered by half-drawn white curtains, catches the gleam of a pearl nested in antique gold on her earlobe and reveals a pale sprinkle of freckles along her cheekbone.

'It's particularly true of the inhabitants of this city, I think, and that has to do with the constant war we wage against the river, which is always seeking to encroach upon us. It's not friendly, we constantly have to push it back, build structures which hold back the water. You'll see it for yourself, as time goes by. We're locked in battle with the very thing which sustains us, gives us life, and that can only have a strange effect on people's psyches.'

Gisèle extracts the new Leica and gazes at this woman who she knows only in the context of the Old World, who spoke French before she learned Spanish. She sees determination, a tightly controlled dominant will; also sensitivity, humour, loneliness. She frames Victoria's face tightly, stops down the aperture to sharpen the depth of field. Her mind previews the image inverted on the focal plane; for a moment her body feels a similar reversal, as though her feet are sticking to the roof of the world.

'Wisdom is a butterfly, not a gloomy bird of prey,' she says, quoting W.B. Yeats. She presses the shutter, even though she knows that the camera has no film, as Victoria turns her face, smiling, away from the window.

'Gisèle! You devil! You sorceress! Look at you, here for five minutes and already you're stealing souls.' Victoria's look is amused, even though her tone reproves. She goes on, more gently, 'You need fattening up. I have roast duck for dinner, vegetables, afterwards, crème caramel, some fine Argentinean wines…'

Gisèle smiles. She puts down the Leica. She recalls a detail from *The lives of the saints*: after her murder, when people came to bury Saint Lucy, they found her eyes miraculously restored.

'I'll eat anything,' she tells her rescuer, 'as long as it's not carrots.'

There are no carrots on the menu that evening and the meal is sumptuous. A brown-skinned woman serves the food. Roger Caillois pours the wine. The light from tall white candles casts fantastic shadows on the wood-panelled walls. In the soft brown luminescence, Gisèle feels like a character from an Ionescu play. Victoria presides, smiling, draped in folds of pewter silk.

Roger Caillois raises his glass to Gisèle: '*Zur glucklichen Ausreise*' –

to a happy emigration – and relates to Victoria the story of Gisèle's almost failed entry to the country. 'I told them you were a cousin of mine, rather dim, almost a halfwit, but with delusions of grandeur.'

They all laugh. Despite her desire to gorge, Gisèle has restricted herself to dainty helpings: she doesn't want to end the first night in her new home by vomiting. She sips her wine and contents herself with listening to Victoria telling Roger Caillois about the difficulties of preparing the latest issue of *Sur*, the literary magazine she owns and edits. *Sur* is a vast sinkhole: so much of Victoria's fortune has gone into financing the venture, to bring discerning readers the best of both European and Latin American writing. Some people would call her a fool but Victoria pursues her vision relentlessly.

'…and of course we must get Gisèle started again.'

Gisèle realises she has been drowsing.

Victoria regards her, smiling, from the end of the long polished table. 'I can introduce you to many people,' she continues, 'those who would be only too happy to have a photographic portrait made by someone as distinguished as yourself.'

Gisèle knows very well that Victoria is gilding the lily. She doubts that anyone in this city would have heard of her. The 1939 exhibition which Adrienne organised was a success but hadn't extended much further than Paris. Anyone who is familiar with her work in Buenos Aires will have doubtless seen it in the papers of *Life* and *Vu*, magazines which must have a very small readership here.

Across the table, Roger Caillois regards her sympathetically, eyes cavernous in the candlelight. 'It may be necessary to seek employment until you establish yourself…'

'Not if I have anything to do about it, but we shall see.' Victoria beckons the maid to clear the table. 'Now, if you'll excuse me…'

Roger Caillois rises as she takes leave to supervise her household. 'Shall we sit outside?'

Gisèle follows him onto the back terrace, which looks out over a wide slope of viridian.

Roger Caillois brings out a small oblong wooden box containing cigarillos which he offers to Gisèle. 'Delicacies from Cuba. Please take one, although it's not done for ladies to smoke them-and it's not done, except in Bohemian circles, for ladies to smoke publicly.'

'My mother always wanted me to be a lady.' Gisèle takes a cigarillo; feels a delicious frisson of transgression as she accepts his light. They sit smoking companionably, watching the pink smoke of sunset. Birds fly to the trees to roost, silent black shapes against the dusk. The membrane of twilight stretches until broken by Roger Caillois.

'Much as I respect Victoria's advice, I would advise you not to take it.' 'Oh?'

'No. You will tire of that clientele very quickly-and you're not suited, as far as your personality goes, to pandering to the rich… You'll in-evitably run up against those with whom you disagree – and, if my memory serves me, you won't be able to remain discreet.'

Gisèle is silent for some time. It is all very well for Roger Caillois to offer advice. A writer only needs a brain, pen and paper as tools of the trade. A photographer has to have camera, lenses and film, access to a dark room. And how was she to afford all those things without first making money? And Victoria's offer of assistance sounded like a way to do it. But she is curious about any alternative Roger Caillois might have. 'Well, what do you suggest I do?'

'Go back to reporting. Get out and explore the country. You need not even stay in Argentina. You have crossed one continent. You can cross another. I have an artist friend in Mexico, Diego Riviera. His wife, Frida Kahlo, also does some painting. I'm sure you would be welcome.'

Gisèle merely feels a leaden weight of exhaustion as he speaks. 'It would be good to settle, good to make some friends.'

'Ah…' Roger Caillios nods. 'You miss Mademoiselle Monnier.'

'I miss many people…' but even as Gisèle says it, those people appear like fragmented figures on a cave wall or smoke from dissolving frames as an old strip of film crackles and burns. Her memory catches hold of them but they slip away. Roger Caillois extinguishes his cigarillo and speaks of

Koestler, Sartre and his erstwhile colleague, Georges Bataille. He recalls visiting Walter Benjamin at an apartment on the rue Bernard in 1937 and seeing the *Novus Angelus* hanging on a stained white plaster wall.

'Lost now,' Gisèle murmurs.

'No,' say Roger Caillois. 'It's hidden in the Bibliotheque Nationale.'

'*What?*' Gisèle stares.

'Just before Benjamin left Paris, he gave it to Bataille – you'll recall he's a librarian there. Bataille hid it in the library.'

'How do you know?'

'Bataille wrote to me, it must have been the last letter to get out of Paris, before the Germans sealed the Occupied Zone. Bataille didn't refer to it by name, of course – he called it the "precious object" – but I knew what he was talking about.'

'Whereabouts in the library did he put it?'

Roger Caillois shrugs. 'Who knows? That Bataille, he's a secretive fellow. He's probably hidden it in some unlikely place, among books about the history of shoes in northern Auvergne…'

'…or seventeenth-century Breton horse breeding…'

'Oh, Breton! What did he ever know, about horse-breeding or anything else?' Roger Caillois had been, for some time before the war, involved with surrealism but, like everyone else, had fallen out with its leader and was thereafter consigned to the outer darkness of his favour. 'I believe he is now in Brazil.'

'Plenty of horse-breeding there!' Their conjectures about André Breton's knowledge of horse breeding become obscene then wildly so. Gisèle laughs, revelling in the delicious silliness of it all. How she has missed this, these jokes and word plays with the people from her world; she had thought she had lost it forever.

Eventually they run out of steam, sit silent again until Roger Caillois yawns, apologises, then gets to his feet. 'Forgive me but it's been a long day. I rose at six this morning.'

'You, who once never got out of bed before ten!'

'It's easier. In the afternoon, the heat prevents you from thinking.'

He indicates the sky. All that remains of the sunset is a murky yellow eye festering in cloud. 'You need to come in, too. It will rain soon.'

Although it is not cold, something about that sky makes Gisèle shiver. 'First rain, then sun. Rain, then sun.'

'You'll get used to it, as you will to many other things. Who knows, you may even come to like soccer.'

'Oh, please!'

In the room which Victoria has prepared for her use, Gisèle arranges the contents of her suitcase and places the new Leica on a lace runner which graces the dressing table. She admires the contrast between the shiny modernity of the camera and the decoration hand-worked by one of Victoria's forebears. Above the camera, a mirror reflects her exhausted face; but the face's eyes look back with a wary optimism.

Gisèle has no time for 'signs' or 'omens' – people who believe in such things are simple-minded – but the knowledge that the *Novus Angelus* survives makes her think that perhaps, after all, Walter Benjamin's work will not be forgotten. Perhaps, after the war, it will be retrieved, along with the aquarelle, now possibly nestled between books on Indian spirituality or horseradish cultivation.

She washes her face in the porcelain bowl of water provided, then lays her clothes on a chair and slips on a calf-length nightdress of white silk. The sensuality of the garment's touch turn her thoughts towards the nearest erotic entanglement: she sees that Roger Caillois is in love but Victoria's emotions are more opaque. Gisèle can't predict how it will finish, only that it will. Even someone like Roger Caillois, worldly and accomplished, can have his heart fractured, if not broken.

Gisèle lies between ironed, sweet-smelling sheets and remembers his kindness and his verbal foolery: she has reason to be grateful. She also has reason to be grateful to the object of their satire, André Breton because if it hadn't been for Breton and his rampaging cohort one afternoon at the Café de Flore, she might not have met Adrienne, and Gisèle cannot imagine a life, a past, without her.

Gisèle smiles. Her eyes close. She sleeps for two days.

He calls her by her name

The Very Grand Lady is not amused.

The tip of her long nose quivers. She looks like an inbred armadillo, Gisèle thinks, armoured as the lady is in stiff gold and midnight-blue brocade and the heavy antique jewels which cover her neck and chest. She holds the black and white photographic prints, which are the source of her displeasure, at arm's length, frowning. Gisèle has not obliterated any of the small scars which mar the lady's cheeks. She did her best with the lighting but it has barely softened her subject's rather corrugated features. Gisèle know that the Very Grand Lady was expecting something different: her own face looks back at her and it is clearly something of a disappointment.

'Madame Ocampo said you were the best in your field.'

The Very Grand Lady speaks French, something Gisèle knows makes her feel cultivated, cosmopolitan. But the lady's accent is thick, almost unintelligible; although they're both speaking the same language, Gisèle struggles to understand her.

Her knowledge of Spanish, however, is growing, so that when the Very Grand Lady sweeps from the room (Gisèle can almost hear the rattle of those ancestral sapphires against the agitated bosom), she is able to partly follow the conversation in the next room which the Very Grand Lady has with Victoria. Words reach Gisèle: 'insulting', 'second-rate' and 'cheated.' She looks at the photographs, which are large black and white prints carefully glazed to a high gloss with a roller after their final fixer bath. Perhaps the face would have been improved if she had used colour film, the cheeks rendered slightly less hollow, the mouth, with its coating of coral-coloured grease, given more generous definition; but 'You can't make a silk purse from a sow's ear.' This is another English expression she learned from Sylvia Beach, in Paris.

Gisèle hears Victoria reply to the voluble stream of complaint in a low soothing tone. She loses the thread of the conversation and gives up trying to understand any more. She looks at the photographs again, at the horsey, not particularly intelligent face and feels a twinge of empathy. Don't we all have some fantasy of beauty which we desire to inhabit? Or, if we don't desire beauty, we want to be 'regal' or 'elegant'. Gisèle thinks back to the way she used to feel when she walked alongside Elsa through the streets of Frankfurt, the admiring glances Elsa would draw with her slender frame, dark blue eyes and yellow hair. Gisèle had felt dark, unseen, the shadowy Shulamith to Elsa's Marguerite.

Victoria enters, looking impossibly *soignée*, as though she was designed for the room, gliding across its black and white marble tiles, a pale pink cashmere cardigan draped across her shoulders. Its colour twins the cashmere sweater and linen skirt she wears.

'Gisèle…' she begins, using the same placating tone she has used with the other woman.

Gisèle seizes the prints and tears them into pieces. She leaves them scattered on the low mahogany coffee table and storms to her room.

Later, on the tram going south, there is a conversation running through her head.

'Must you always make things difficult for yourself, Gisèle?'

'Truth is important. I will not compromise…'

'Yes, but *why*? Why is it so important to you?'

Even now, this is an answer she cannot fully articulate. The integrity of the image: bah! She knows all about that. A photo she had taken of the Bourse in 1935 had been used, with completely different headlines, in a Belgian and then a German paper. In Belgium, there had been 'Rise on the Paris Stock Exchange. Shares reaching fabulous prices'; but in Germany it was another story: 'Panic in the Paris Stock Exchange. Fortunes topple. Thousands ruined.' A photograph is infinitely corruptible, able to be manipulated first one way, then another. Even a portrait can be changed, embellished, given beauty which is skin deep.

It is difficult not to be corrupted by this process, especially when there is money involved (and there is always money involved).

One day, Gisèle thinks, she should write something about this.

The streets pass her by, still exacting in their strangeness. The tram is full; people stand in the aisle. A large man looms above, breathing down something alcoholic. The woman next to her gradually eases her considerable bulk along the seat until Gisèle is squashed to the side of the tram. She considers asking the woman to move but can't remember the right words. She will just have to accept it, as she has learned to accept most everyday occurrences here.

She has got used to the turbulence of the traffic, of having to almost batter her way through the waves of pedestrians which approach. The riotous vegetation, the flowers which constantly explode into bloom, is something which excites her eye but the noise, the constant unrelenting clamour grinds her nerves. She has always thought of herself as an urban creature, has never sought out a pastoral retreat. Nevertheless, she has come to regard the many parks which dot the city as oases of quiet; as the tram arrives at the corner Florida Street and Avenue Santa Fe, she is tempted to step off and walk in the shade of trees which pre-date the Spanish arrival.

But she leaves her decision too late; by the time she has pushed her way to the door, the tram has finished disgorging passengers to the department stores of Florida Street and moved on. Gisèle stands, swaying, while fragments of her surrounds blur past. She can't see the docks which sprawl endlessly on her left, kilometre after kilometre of squat buildings which police the sullen river but there's a fleeting triangular snippet of the post office, there's the US embassy, very close to the Casa Rosada (convenient, Gisèle thinks ironically) and the offices which house various government ministries.

As the tram nears the Avenue Mexico, a cumbersome, many-fronted tan building beckons her.

'Corner!' yells Gisèle, determined not to be left behind this time, and the tram obediently slows to a stop. She gets down and walks across the avenue to the public library.

For some minutes, she just sits there, savouring the cool and the quiet, feeling as though she has reached a pool of still water. She thinks of all the libraries in which she has spent time, in Berlin, Frankfurt and Paris. She'd wanted to be a sociologist: if there hadn't been such a powerful need to earn her living, she would have had a career as a scholar. Not that she regrets the path necessity forced her down…

Gisèle realises she is being stared at by several pairs of eyes from across the open area of long wooden tables where she has chosen to sit. She can't just sit here; she will have to do something.

'Fotografia?' She asks the librarian on duty, who is slim, dapper, with dark liquid eyes and close-cropped hair (how René Crevel would have loved him!).

He directs her to the second floor.

When Gisèle steps from the lift, it takes her some time to find what she wants. She walks between the rows of towering metal shelves, seeking methodically. There's a folio written in Cyrillic script, its cover adorned with the face of a grimy-faced miner, and when she pulls it out and carries it to a desk, she smiles in recognition. Here is Alexander Rodchenko, here is Abram Petrovich Sterenberg, here is Mikhail Nappelbaum; here are Otsup, Bulla and Zhukov: the heroes of Soviet photography. Gisèle pages slowly through Rodchenko's experiments with photomontage, which leave her cold, but she delights in his cityscape taken on the diagonal: the image shows a solitary woman, shadow behind her, traversing a white tier of steps, child in arms.

This had been the challenge, earlier in the century: to capture the speed of modern life, the fragmentation of a building glimpsed from a passing tram; to invent new subjects and ways of seeing for new societies. There had been such dynamism and energy in those early years after the Revolution, before the dead hand of socialist realism pushed it all down.

Still… Gisèle lingers over Sterenberg's portraits, a Mongolian wearing a flat circular hat of fur, his face creased above a scrawny salt-and-pepper beard; a violinist, hands blurred, face intent upon his instrument. Gisèle has read somewhere that Sterenberg never retouches his photos and, remembering the contretemps earlier in the day, feels kinship and repect.

There are, of course, multiple portraits of Lenin. Gisèle skims through them until she comes to the photo of the Bolshevik revolutionary addressing troops in 1920, taken by G.P. Goldshtein. Gisèle looks for the lieutenants, Trotsky and Kamenev, who she knows are pictured in the original, but they're not there: Comrade Stalin has taken care of that. It is the fate of Trotsky and Kamenev to be erased from history by the very regime they helped found. Despite her knowledge of what has happened in the Soviet Union and her cynicism regarding the uses to which photography is used as propaganda and misinformation, Gisèle feels a chill. She replaces the book on its shelf.

Is there no one who can give her any clues or show her direction? Perhaps new ideas can only come from within. Gisèle takes down a folio printed in Spanish containing some of Tina Modotti's portraits; she has never seen the Italian woman's work, although she knows it by reputation. Initially, she feels excited when she sees these photos: here is a European woman with the courage to pioneer a new country, an alien culture, Mexico, during the 1920s.

She looks at Modotti's strong-featured men and women but is particularly impressed by *Mexican peasant boy*, taken in 1927. The child's sturdy features gaze back impassively at the viewer, framed by the sombrero he wears. There might almost be something sentimental here, some homage to the labouring classes but Gisèle sees the silvery line of disease at the base of the boy's right eye, a thread of infection caused by inadequate diet and poor sanitation. How clever to show but not tell, to leave the deciphering to the viewer. She knows that Modotti was a hard-line Stalinist who was active in the Spanish Civil War but, in spite of being so blinkered in some ways, this woman, recently dead in rather mysterious circumstances, was a true artist.

She is less enamoured by Diego Rivera's murals, which Modotti recorded and also feature in the book. Where is the demarcation line between propaganda and art? Is there any real difference, in terms of purpose, between Rivera's flat-featured workers wearing overalls and holding hammers, and the religious iconography of medieval European frescos?

Gisèle closes the book without reaching any conclusions. She's beginning to feel thirsty and hungry. In the drama involving the Very Grand Lady, she somehow missed breakfast this morning.

She is just about to leave when a title in German catches her eye. She takes it down and sees some of Germaine Krull's work. Gisèle flicks past Krull's industrial monuments, the images of pylons and pistons, girders and gyrospheres. She looks with some nostalgia at a street scene, cars converging at Place de l'Étoile and at the lion crouched in front of the obelisk at the Place de la Concorde but then she stops her indifferent turning for there is the young (or at least youngish) Walter Benjamin, gaze fixed eternally inward, shadowy hand holding a cigarette. (Krull had a thing about hands, Gisèle recalls, believed they were a great psychological indicator; in this way, she was like one of those Soviets, Mikahil Nappelbaum.)

She is suddenly jealous, comparing the 1926 portrait with her own, taken twelve years later, when Benjamin was an émigré in Paris. Krull has captured Benjamin's yearning, melancholic nature; her own photograph, made in 1938, shows him middle-aged, pudgy and defensive-looking. His right hand is sharply focused and held to his face protectively. It is as though Walter was barricading himself against all that had beset him since 1933: poverty, homelessness, professional ostracism. Photographs can show an absence, Gisèle thinks: what should have been, what might have been.

She closes the book. How strange it is that she and Krull never crossed paths, either in Germany or later, in Paris. From what she can gather, allowing for the fact that much of the little she knows about Krull's life is gossip and hearsay, there are some similarities between that life and her own. Gisèle glimpsed Germaine once, in 1935, driving an open-topped car down the Boulevard Saint-Germain while giving the world an indiscriminate gap-toothed smile. She has seen Krull's photograph of a nude woman in a field, recalls the erotic thrill that the combination of beauty and power gave her.

Gisèle sneezes, once, then again. The musty old book smell clogs her nostrils. She must get out of here. She leaves the book on the desk and walks to the lift. Downstairs, the beautiful young librarian has been replaced by a middle-aged peroxided woman wearing pince-nez.

A white blaze of noonday sun blinds Gisèle as she steps onto the street. She's light-headed from her time spent sitting down, dazed by the heat and unceasing clamour. She buys a pasty filled with vegetables and meat, a local food she's comes to enjoy and one she was surprised to find here, thinking that the English had a monopoly on this stodgy item. She drinks at a public fountain then walks on to the Plaza de Congresco, where she sits and watches the ornate fountains in front of the Argentine Congress.

The sun makes her drowsy, on the low stone bench where she sits. The clear spill of water, sheened with rainbow, becomes a transparent veil between one world and another so she thinks she must have fallen into a dream when she hears a voice calling, 'Zelli! Zelli!'

The voice is familiar, heard a long time ago, but thickened and muffled, some sort of echoing aberration.

'Zelli! Zelli!'

Gisèle starts and looks around but there is no one there, just a cripple in a wheelchair being pushed by an old man. The cripple also appears retarded. His mouth is a ragged hole; he wears a protective leather helmet of the type worn by epileptics. He sways and beats at the air with hands which are subhuman paws.

'Zelli! Zelli!'

Gisèle watches them approach, transfixed with incomprehension.

The old man pushes the chair towards her and halts with obvious relief inside the arc of shade where she sits. 'Gisèle,' he says gently. 'It is so good to see you. Since the day when I told you to leave, I've been worried.' Then, seeing her continued bafflement, 'It's Wilhelm von Eckersdorf and Gerhard.'

As the words fall from his lips, Gisèle recognises Herr Professor von Eckersdorf, that exalted figure in the Frankfurt law faculty, distant and revered, an expert in jurisprudence. Even now, though his face is lined and his black hair patched with white, she can still find traces of the proud austerity which marked him and made him such a formidable adversary for his son; but she knows, now, on any street, she would not have recognised him .

'May I sit down?' The professor's Old World courtesy has not deserted him.

'Of course…' Gisèle gathers her wits and her manners, although it is difficult to take her eyes off the creature in the wheelchair.

It waves its arms and makes sounds which are somewhere between a groan and a splutter. From a small bag attached to the back of the wheelchair, his father hands him a sky-blue woollen bear, the sort of thing you would give an infant. His son takes it, smiles, coos at the toy.

'That is good. You play with Bruno.' His father watches for a few moments then turns his attention back to Gisèle.

'And how is your family? Did they manage to escape?'

'They're in England. They left not long after I did.'

'Ah, that's good, that's good. Julius could always see ahead.'

Gisèle does not bother to tell him how her parents managed it. Like so many other of the *haute bourgeoisie*, they had disdained the National Socialists and had not thought it possible that they would ever take power. She imagines that Wilhelm, who was openly contemptuous of 'the masses' and who detested his son's involvement with the left, had felt very much the same.

Gisèle contains these memories and instead gives him a brief and edited account of her life over the last ten years. She has just reached the crossing to Buenos Aires when Gerhard suddenly abandons the blue bear and fixes her with the one eye not coated with scar tissue.

'Zelli has a dress with swans on it.'

Wilhelm's smile has a pleading edge. 'He sometimes imagines things…'

'No, he's right,' says Gisèle. 'It was the dress I was wearing the last time h–' she stumbles, trying to say the name, 'Gerhard saw me.'

The day of the demonstration, she would have preferred trousers, so much easier to move about in, but they marked her as unconventional, even deviant, and thus made her an easy target for those men who believed that women belonged solely in the spheres of kitchen and nursery. She had worn that green dress, loose-fitting and patterned with small white swans, instead.

The old man watches his son take up the blue bear again. 'He still has flashes of cognition. And it was he who saw you first –'

Gisèle is silent. She could walk away. She could disclaim any desire to return to that time. She knows she is about to hear a story she does not want to hear, the story which is proof of defeat and destruction. In spite of this, she waits for the professor to speak.

He gestures to the helmeted man, now uttering those same incoherent sounds. 'This is what happened on the day I warned you to leave.'

'During the rally?'

'Yes, that. The brown shirts had taken his sweetheart, Bertha –'

'Elsa.'

'Elsa.' The Herr Professor smiles sadly. 'You understand, Gerhard and I were estranged at the time and that I never met the young lady. From what I can gather, from what some of his friends told me later, Gerhard went to intercede with her captors…'

'Yes,' says Gisèle, falling off a precipice to realisation. 'I glimpsed him talking to two of them.'

'They called some of their comrades and set upon him. Several people tried to help but they were outnumbered and unarmed.'

The sun, moving across the afternoon sky, has bared the patch of grass on which the wheelchair rests.

Gerhard's father stands, pushes it carefully into the sanctuary of shade. 'He was taken to hospital. For some time, it was unclear whether he would live. By the time he had recovered, as much as he was going to recover, I had been removed from my position at the university. Things were hard for us. We were not able to depart until 1937. We could have gone to the United States but my wife and I thought the climate would better suit our son.'

Gisèle recalls Frau von Eckersdorf, a plump, softly spoken woman who dressed in expensive clothes of subdued shades.

'My wife died not long after we arrived. The doctors said cancer…' the Herr Professor pauses for a moment, '…that is what they put it down to. Since then, I have managed more or less on my own. Family and friends send me money…'

'That is always a great help.' How banal it sounds, 'a great help,' but if it hadn't been for the money her parents sent her, she would have starved in Paris.

Gisèle watches scenes of everyday life go on around her: a girl of three or four, wearing an elaborately smocked cream and yellow dress, evades her mother's clutches and runs towards the waterfall, heedless of the anxious cries pursuing her; young lovers stroll hand in hand, oblivious to everyone. But that's how it is: even though the sky falls in for some, those who are not affected go on as usual.

For several minutes, she and the Herr Professor are silent, while the man in the wheelchair croons to his toy.

'It was my nephew who betrayed the group,' Herr von Eckersdorf says eventually. 'We found that out some time later. For some time, he had been in the pay of the…'

'Of course.' It seems obvious now. Of course, it was Johannes, Johannes who looked so like Gerhard but was always a younger, paler version of his charismatic cousin, so easily overlooked. Was that why he had betrayed his own blood? Was it simple jealousy or a bid for attention, rather than ideological fervour? No matter: whatever the motivation, the outcome would have been the same. Did he see Elsa's coffin? Did he weep?

'My brother financed our exit from Germany.' Herr von Eckersdorf smiles ironically. 'I think he felt we were owed that much. But I have spent so much time telling you my troubles… You plan to return to Europe after the war?'

'Who can make plans?' Gisèle smiles and makes a brief dismissive gesture, hoping to deflect further conversation in this direction. Her own future is so uncertain and clearly anything to do with plans is not a question she can put to Herr von Eckersdorf; but she is saved from having to elaborate any of this because Gerhard, hitherto quiet, suddenly launches into a tirade of abuse against his woolly companion.

'Bad! Bad! Bad! Bad Bruno! Bad!' He strikes the bear repeatedly then attempts to twist off its head.

His father watches this frenzy quite calmly. 'It's time we went home for our nap.' Disregarding the flailing arms, he takes the bear from his son, who subsides and begins rubbing the front of his trousers. Equally calmly, the Herr Professor moves the hand and speaks as though he were in a drawing room in Frankfurt. 'Please don't. You are embarrassing the young lady.' He turns to Gisèle. 'Will you do something for me?'

'Of course.'

'I want you to photograph Gerhard. I want to show the world what those scum are capable of. There is an émigré paper here…'

Something shifts in the pit of Gisèle's stomach. She watches as he takes paper and pen (surprisingly, a modern ballpoint) and writes down an address and phone number in a nineteenth-century script of loops and curlicues.

'Please phone us sometime.' He proffers it to her with a small half-bow.

This is the man who saved her life: to show him pity would be to belittle him. Cravenly, Gisèle takes the slip of paper. The Herr Professor turns the wheelchair towards the south of the city, where Gisèle has never been.

The Herr Professor half-turns then looks back. 'Gerhard used to speak about you, quite often, before we became estranged, with a great deal of affection and respect. He always thought there was something special about you, that you would make your mark.'

'Perhaps, one day.' Gisèle smiles at them both. 'Goodbye for now.'

'Goodbye, Zelli.' Gerhard gives her a smart salute. He takes the arm of the bear, with whom he is apparently on good terms again, and waves it, behaving like a charming five-year-old.

What else can Gisèle do but wave back? 'Zelli': besides her father, the only people who ever called her that were the members of the Frankfurt group. The wrecked man in the wheelchair remembers. Does he remember Elsa, slender, delicate, wearing a dress of black crêpe which he laughingly derided as 'fit only for an old lady' while his eyes paid homage to her elegance? Gerhard: tall, ruddy-cheeked, virile; he could have modelled for a National Socialist recruitment poster.

Gisèle sits for a long time, oblivious to the shops and offices reopening after siesta. She remembers the green dress, utterly inadequate against the frigid sky with its threat of snow, worn only to remind Elsa, if their paths crossed, that they had bought it together one afternoon. They had entered the shop and spent the entire time laughing together as they tried on all kinds of clothes which were either utterly inappropriate or too expensive, attempting to goad the thin-lipped sales assistant past the limit of her patience. She had been wearing it when she fled, the roll of film strapped to her ribcage beneath its blowsy folds.

'They're looking for you,' the Herr Professor had said when Gisèle had hurried back to the university after finishing the last film and he did not need to tell her who 'they' were. 'Have you seen my son? Was he there? His mother is worried…'

'No, I haven't seen him.' Gisèle had been barely conscious of her lie, already in flight to the railway station, bag slung over her shoulder. 'You need to ask his girlfriend or Johannes.' But by then, Elsa was in the hands of the barbarians and Johannes had already slipped away, out of the picture.

Because this is what had happened: she, of all people had misread the picture. She had let jealousy corrode her vision. What would have happened if she had stayed instead of turning away? Could she have called for help, fled to rally support before the thugs inflicted their violence? Gisèle can't tell. She only knows that Gerhard was a sacrifice, a victim, like Elsa, like Walter, like all the others.

The light has begun to fade. There is a man hovering nearby who winks at her lasciviously. Gisèle swears at him in Spanish – that much of the language she has learned – but she knows it is time to get moving. She rises and begins to walk in the direction of the tram line, passing though the crowds who have come out to enjoy the evening. What happened to that green dress in Paris? She tries to remember. She thinks it may have been lost during one of her moves during the difficult early years.

As she crosses Cerrito Lima, she takes the piece of paper with the phone number on it, tears it into pieces and throws it on the ground. A silver-grey pigeon, weary, short-sighted, soon to fly roostwards, swoops down, thinking it is food.

'Take a gun'

When she arrives back at Palermo Chico, Roger Caillois is ensconced in the drawing room behind a month-old French newspaper.

He raises an eyebrow as Gisèle enters. 'Is it possible our esteemed photographer has begun to suffer from memory lapses caused by the onset of old age?'

'I beg your pardon.'

'Olivia phoned. She's rather put out you didn't meet her –'

'Oh, hell! Damn it!' Gisèle has forgotten all about Olivia, who she was meant to meet an hour ago at a bar for drinks and then, possibly dinner. Too late now: all she can do is phone and apologise, hoping that this tentative friendship won't be nipped in the bud before it flowers.

Roger Caillois regards her sympathetically. 'I know that you've had a rather difficult day.'

Gisèle gives a slight start then realises he is referring to the early encounter with the Very Grand Lady, something she has forgotten completely. Now, she fastens on it, as a way of avoiding having to think about her two maimed countrymen. 'It was a mistake to think I could succeed with her, or indeed with anyone like her.'

He flexes the flimsy pages in his hands as though he would strangle the entire Argentine upper class. 'Why concern yourself with these tired old parasites? You have better things to do.'

'I've been thinking that I might travel…' Actually, Gisèle hadn't realised this, until the words come out of her mouth.

'By all means travel: that's what I've already advised – but take a gun when you do.'

'Naturally,' says Gisèle. Naturally, take a gun. That way, she might be outnumbered but will never be unarmed. She leaves him to dissect Vichy's lies and goes to phone Olivia.

Later, in her room, after she has told the maid she will not be down to dinner, bathed in the warmth of Olivia's reassurances, Gisèle meditates on jealousy, the disease that is the craving to be best-loved. She sits at a small white table by a window which is blocked with panes of thick occluded glass, one of Victoria's Art Deco eccentricities in an otherwise nineteenth-century room, through which moonlight seeps, cracked and wavering. The blind nebulous faces of white flowers loom through the darkness.

Gisèle knows that Olivia has a lover, a man; she also knows that a tension exists between herself and Olivia that she, Gisèle, may choose to act on, or not. Whatever happens, she must not turn the situation into a competition. She has a sudden great need to break her silence about these things, to lay bare the behaviour which clouded her vision, but she can't speak of this to Roger or Victoria; there is only one person, no, two people, who would fully understand. From the one drawer of the table she takes out writing materials, silky paper lined with pale blue, a fountain pen and ink. She dips the nib into the bottle and makes a few experimental scratches.

Gerhard, Johannes, Elsa, Gabriela, Magdalena, Christophe, Ulrich, Theo, Trudi... The names slide across her mind like a linkage of beads strung on fine wire. Gisèle struggles to recall the other two but they have become phantoms, shadowy traces without definition, like the faint markings on a sheet of photographic paper exposed too soon to the light, with its image stillborn. Perhaps, one day, they will all have vanished and, when that happens, the memory of their ludicrous courage will also be extinguished.

Gisèle begins a letter which will never be sent. Tomorrow she will apologise to Victoria for causing her potential embarrassment, although Gisèle knows that Victoria is really too wealthy and important to have her social standing dented by what has occurred. She will be gracious, even amused, probably tell Gisèle that the Very Grand Lady is someone she has always detested.

…and so you see, this is something I will always carry as a burden, the knowledge that I should have seen better, been better. Atonement is very important to the Jewish people: in the religion of my ancestors, in which I was not raised, Yom Kippur is one of the High Holy Days, the time when a person dresses in white and fasts (doesn't even drink water) while they seek forgiveness from God for their sins. But it is too late for me for God. All I can do is keep on recording the events of our time, to offer up these moments of frozen light, to try to see better, be better. To try to say: This is how it was.

I have so much to thank you for. You led me through the maze of French bureaucracy when the Leica had got me into all kinds of trouble. (Those men who thought I was spying for the Germans! They must have been insane. Nevertheless, that's what they thought.) And your idea to hold a show of my colour portraits saved me; without that exhibition, I would have continued scrabbling for whatever scraps the magazines would throw me, shitty work advertising cosmetics or foundation garments. After the exhibition they took me more seriously (although not as seriously as Germaine Krull or André Kertesz.) Remember Valéry and Joyce comparing notes, each saying that the other's portrait was a good likeness while dismissing their own. Yes, it is strange what people see.

And, more than anyone, you were my home in Paris. The hours spent discussing literature, cooking dinner in the apartment, dazzling me with those people who had just been names to me but who took on flesh and blood around the table or in front of the stove in your shop: looking back I cringe a little, to think of my occasionally over-exuberant displays; but it was just a cover for awe. You completed what my father began in Berlin in the far-off days before that country became infected with its current disease.

Perhaps when the war is over and I have returned to France we will walk once more down the Boulevard Raispail and I will buy you smoky-pink tulips, like the ones you bought on that day in 1935, after Breton and his cronies knocked me down in the Flore. Until then take care and please pass on my affection and respect to Sylvia. I wasn't always considerate of her feelings, a bit of a brat, really, grabbing without thinking, but I was in love, if that can ever be used as a reason to justify anything…

When the pages are complete, Gisèle sets them aside. She is weary to the bone and, more than anything, wants to sleep without dreaming. She rises, taking the letter with her. Tomorrow, she will visit the offices of *Life* magazine.

The light at the edge of the sky

Roger Caillois, that soft-palmed intellectual, has found Gisèle a gun. 'Just point it and fire,' he suggests, when she asks him how to use it.

Gisèle aims it playfully, cowboy and Indian style, which causes an expression of alarm to cross his face. 'This is what I used to wish for in the Tiergarten, when my brother would tease me to tears,' she says. 'What a pity he's somewhere else now!'

She and Roger Caillois both laugh.

It is barely morning. All through the night, there have been cold explosions of rain which have left an early morning glisten on the streets of Nequen but here, in this semi-rural slum on the town's outskirts, there is a muddy yard and moving shapes which emerge from the murky light to become mules and two sullen Indian men clad in woven woollen capes, trousers and worn boots. Behind them, a white man gives orders in Spanish then turns to the Indian woman who accompanies them, a mestizo baby strapped to her back.

Gisèle rises and approaches her, smiling, but the woman sees the Leica and flees, head down. The three men take no notice, although the Spaniard barks something at her, in a tone you would use to order a dog.

Gisèle puts the camera away. She is almost glad to have an excuse because, contrary to her best intentions, she stayed up late last night and consequently the raw edge of alcohol had its teeth into her sleep. She rarely drinks to excess but the sight of Victoria, immaculately groomed even here, and pouring out tall glasses of champagne from the back seat of the long car which transported them, makes her wish she had stuck to her guns and arrived alone.

Gisèle stamps her feet to warm them. She is dressed in layers against the raw air, woollen jacket then sweater, shirt and undershirt. Oh, the glory of wearing trousers again, without having to endure the stares and censorious comments that this would have inevitably drawn in the city. Here it might only be regarded by her travelling companions as foreign eccentricity, not a kind of flaunting perversity. The last week has been full of planning and acquisition and organising transport. Victoria's friends, the owners of the enormous ranch at which she, Roger Caillois and Gisèle have been guests, have supplied the necessary guide and cook and given him the requested pistol.

This flurry of organisation, the need to consider stocks of flour and consult maps has barricaded Gisèle against recalling recent events. For the first few days after her encounter with Gerhard and his father, she had had dreams in which Elsa appeared, a blonde ghost running ahead of her down a street blocked at the end with something dark, hulking and anonymous. Last week, after leaving the Museum of History in Leama Park, Gisele had stopped suddenly before the shallow pool over which twin elegant jets of water played, because she had seen a man parked in a wheelchair. She had hurried towards him, calling out, only to have him turn his head and reveal someone elderly, neatly dressed and carrying a bag of breadcrumbs with which to feed some gathering ducks.

'What on earth were you thinking?' Roger Caillois had asked, looking at her with a combination of amusement and perplexity, for Gisèle had been trembling, almost incoherent, gabbling an apology.

All through that week, until she had heard from *Life*, giving her the go ahead, Gisèle had felt as though she was imprisoned in a cage between past and future, unable to go forward, not wanting to go back.

'Senorita, Madame wishes you to join her.'

It is Fani, Victoria's maid, summoning her. Reluctantly, Gisèle follows her to the Daimler. She knows from past experience that there will be a luxurious picnic laid out: caviar, cheeses and pâté, truffles sliced paper-thin and wedges of melon, pawpaw and grapes. Gisèle dawdles, not because she wants to postpone parting but because the thought of facing such a sybaritic spread revolts her. She is suddenly glad that for the next weeks or months her diet will be barely more than subsistence: water, or coffee brewed above a fire, processed dried beef and hard biscuits, perhaps the occasional meal of hunted meat.

She wishes for some excuse to delay but the clouds bunching overhead and the cold slice of wind, make her increase her pace. The temperature drops, hail spatters briefly and the maid and waiting chauffeur take refuge in a nearby shed. Gisèle flings herself against the beige leather seats, shaking ice from her hair, accepting the glass which Victoria hands her. For several minutes, there is a white haze of rain then the rising sun bursts hotly through the banks of cloud. Suddenly, the sky is banded with yellow, orange, red, green, blue, indigo and violet.

'See,' says Victoria, 'a good omen for your journey. The rainbow is God's promise, or, if you want to be pagan, the necklace worn by the Babylonian goddess Ishtar.'

'Actually, it's sunlight which bends when entering a raindrop and reflects at a right angle off its inside wall then bends again when it exits,' Gisèle tells her. The Dom Perignon is acid on her tongue, souring her response.

'Please don't destroy my poetic illusions with scientific facts.' Victoria laughs then raises her glass. 'Well, here's wishing you well, all the way to Tierra del Fuego!'

'I don't know whether I'll get that far south.'

Sensing tension, Roger Caillois makes his own toast. 'Wherever you go, carry your camera like a conquistador!'

Gisèle grimaces. Briefly, the violated face of the Indian woman rises before her eyes. Abruptly, she opens the car door and walks away, tipping the alcohol on the ground as she goes. She sees Victoria open her mouth to speak; sees Roger Caillois put a hand on her arm, silencing her.

Gisèle leaves them to be a murmuring lover's knot. She is bored with couples. Even her leave-taking from Olivia had been relatively painless, lunch at a favourite café, admiring the new blouse, a white crêpe de Chine patterned with red cherries then cheek kissing and warm assurances that she would be in touch on her return. What a contrast to her leave-taking from Adrienne at the Gare de l'Austerlitz; but then, she has every confidence that she will see Olivia again.

Gisèle remembers that day in 1940, the weather incongruously sunny and warm, a breeze lifting grit from the platform, people jostling for tickets then fighting each other for seats, the swirl and surge of a terrified populace. She had been lucky: when the Germans had broken through the Maginot Line, she had cabled her parents, who sent the money for her escape.

'Remember, your material will be quite safe with me,' Adrienne had assured her, gazing up at the corridor of the third-class carriage to which Gisèle was consigned.

'Burn it, if you have to. Don't take chances.'

'Take good care of yourself.' Adrienne's eyes were swimming lakes. The first time Gisèle had ever seen her cry; for all her sensitivity, Adrienne is rarely captive to emotional overflow.

Gisèle reached one arm through an open window just as the whistle for departure sounded. The train shuddered, clanked; began to move. Adrienne's hand, outstretched through the throng, had tried to make contact but the crowd had been too dense. As the train picked up speed for its journey south, her last farewell had been lost.

Neither had known that the Germans would take the plum of Paris and isolate it from a large part of France, cutting the country in two and making communication almost impossible. Gisèle knows that she owes her life to Adrienne, that she survived long enough to contact Victoria; beyond that, silence.

Gisèle shivers: the wind has increased in strength and bows down the few scrubby trees nearby. It may bring more rain before the day is out and slow down her expedition, which will travel almost due south, along a trail used by traders and adventurers. Sometimes they will stop at towns, sometimes bypass civilisation to make camp on the endless plain.

The idea of this stretching openness daunts and excites Gisèle simultaneously. Ahead, the great steppe, criss-crossed east–west by gleaming stretches of water strung around the southern part of the continent like jewels around the throat of a temptress; beyond that, a confluence of oceans, the salty roil of the Pacific, the Southern and the Atlantic; and always, as she journeys towards land's end, the Andes, rising on her distant right.

Gisèle looks in the direction of these mountains and is reminded, suddenly and unwillingly, of the Pyrenees.

She can't look back. If she looks back, she will see Walter Benjamin.

'Gisèle! Gisèle! What are you doing? Are you intending to walk the entire distance?'

It is Roger Caillois calling and beckoning. Gisèle turns back, surprised at how far she has wandered. Roger Caillois is out of breath, slimy curls of mud adhere to his shoes and a lock of hair has fallen across his forehead. Gisèle is rather pleased at having disturbed his cosmopolitan surface but she follows docilely enough, back to where Victoria waits by the car. They embrace, careful with each other to the end, a warm relationship striated by privilege and obligation.

The overseer and two Indians have entrained. When Gisèle attempts to mount the remaining saddled mule, it turns its head and bites her.

'Swine!' Gisèle smacks it across the nose and swears at it in German, to which Roger Caillois grins and says, 'No, Gisèle, it's a mule.'

'I don't care what it is! She must learn to do what I want her to do!'

'And it's not a "she",' Victoria calls. 'Mules aren't male or female, they're some kind of third sex.'

'Oh, appropriate,' snaps Gisèle. She turns the stubborn beast, lurches in the saddle and almost falls.

Roger Caillois and Victoria lean against the car and laugh until the tears come.

The overseer dismounts, not laughing, annoyed at this delay. 'Here, here. I tie you.' He fastens Gisèle's ankles around the beast, binding her in a way that feels both secure and vulnerable.

'You could always take the car, you know,' says Victoria, recovering from her hilarity.

'Yes, but I wouldn't see as much from a car,' and further south many of the roads become impassable to vehicles, certainly the type of vehicle Victoria is willing to loan.

The brief from *Life* had been surprisingly elastic, 'a portrait of a nation'. How to portray a nation, wonders Gisèle, as she tightens her canvas waterproof coat around her. What faces represent it: the poet, the demagogue, the artisan, the whore? All she knows is that she is determined not to sink into cliché or take the well-travelled road. No smiling girls in ruffled skirts or strutting gauchos for her: she will explore the byways, the backwaters; uncover the unseen.

She flicks the reins. The mule flicks its ears then cooperates. Roger Caillois and Victoria wave goodbye.

'Send us a postcard!' Roger Caillois calls, to which Gisèle responds with one of the Spanish oaths with which she has become familiar.

The overseer in front turns his head briefly, looking startled that a woman such as herself would know this expression.

Gisèle laughs. She thinks about languages, that they are a country a person can inhabit, as comfortably as a citizen or as uneasily as a refugee. For her, there is German, which she may never speak again (anyway, not if she can help it); French acquired haphazardly on the streets and in bed; snatches of English taken from the unemployed men and women she photographed in the northern cities in 1936. (When she photographed Virginia Woolf several years later, she had found it almost impossible to understand Woolf's strangulated upper-middle class voice; had understood her frailty and despair, though.)

Perhaps, Gisèle thinks, looking up to the sky where the clouds are thinning and some kind of small crested raptors wheel and swoop against subtle pools of light, she will never be fluent or easy in any language, always a woman far from home. She accepts this idea without self-pity or melodrama, formed as she is by the events of her century: an exile, a refugee, a survivor

She is travelling light, a necessity on this journey but perhaps another characteristic born of her history. Besides the pistol, she has packed a change of clothes, a compass and an extra pair of boots. She has taken no books except a notebook which may end up being part diary, part natural history record. Tucked away in a small leather pouch are her identity papers, the letter from *Life* magazine signed by its photographic editor and a single photograph.

It's very small, an oblong of a few centimetres with an old-fashioned, deckled edge. It shows a young woman, slight and fair, sitting on a coat which is spread on grass in a park of some kind: there are shrubs behind her which feature white blobs of flowers. The girl wears a light cotton dress, low shoes and a cardigan. Her blonde hair is caught back on the nape of her neck and flares in a nimbus behind her. (The negative was slightly overexposed and this defect was not corrected at the commercial printers where the roll of film was sent.) Her features are blurry – she has turned her head away just at the moment shutter flicked up, as though to avert a blow. Even people who knew her well would have difficulty recognising who it was. Indeed, when Gisèle looked at the snapshot before packing it away, she almost had to remind herself that this was Elsa, photographed on a long-ago spring day in Berlin, when neither of them could be bothered with school. They had made an impromptu picnic of bread and cheese and fruit then Gisèle had picked up the new Leica, her sixteenth-birthday gift from Julius.

This is what photographs do: they carry the slippage of time, the burden of history which is capable of turning grief into mere nostalgia, the lust for a past always remembered as Arcadia. The moment which the camera arrests becomes banal and turns the beloved face to a cipher, remote as a talismanic angel in a painting.

Gisèle turns to give a last farewell to the people who have sheltered and protected her but they have dwindled, almost lost to sight, obscured by a curtain of misty air. The figures riding ahead of her, dissolve, reappear, dissolve. She feels marooned, lost in the vastness of an alien place. The sullen beast beneath her exhales small clouds of vapour as it plods on until suddenly the sun strikes through once more. The landscape takes on form and mass and ahead, barely visible, is the horizon, with its traitor light, pure, elusive, dissolving eternally, a chimera which travels before her: her homeland.

Author's note

Most of the characters depicted in *The Light at the Edge of the Sky* existed in history, and the events described in the novel also have a basis in fact. However, some details have been compressed or changed slightly to achieve greater narrative coherence. There is no evidence that the German officer who entered Sylvia Beach's shop, Shakespeare & Company, late in 1941, knew Gisèle Freund. Freund was a member of an anti-fascist group when she was a student in Frankfurt and she also escaped the invading Germans by fleeing first to the south of France and thence to Argentina; however, the details of these events are entirely my invention.

The triangular relationship which existed for some time between Adrienne Monnier, Sylvia Beach and Gisèle Freund was something none of the three women ever spoke or wrote about except, occasionally, in terms of 'friendship'; this, despite the erotic connection between Monnier and Beach, and Monnier and Freund which was known to their contemproaries. Once again, the descriptions in the novel are a work of my own imagination.

For historical background, I have relied primarily on *The Very Rich Hours of Adrienne Monnier*, Charles Scribner, New York, 1976; Noel Riley Fitch's excellent *Sylvia Beach and the lost generation: a history of literary Paris in the twenties and thirties*, Penguin, London, 1983; and Gisèle Freund's memoir, *The World in My Camera*, Dial, New York, 1974, which, like most memoirs, conceals as much as it reveals.

Many books assisted me in understanding the time of the German Occupation of Paris, particularly Ronald Rosbottom's *When Paris Went Dark: the City of Light under German Occupation*, John Murray, London, 2014; and Simone de Beauvoir's *The Prime of Life*, Penguin, London, 1989. For the life of Walter Benjamin, I have been guided by Howard Eiland and Michael W. Jennings, *Walter Benjamin: a critical life,* Belknap, Cambridge, Massachusetts; London, 2014. Any historical inaccuracies or blunders are my own.

Adrienne Monnier

Due to ill health, Monnier sold her bookshop in the early 1950s, although she continued to write and publish criticism and essays. She was eventually diagnosed with Ménières disease and, increasingly debilitated, committed suicide in 1955 by taking an overdose of barbiturates.

Sylvia Beach

Beach was interned by the Germans for six months in 1942 but eventually released. After the war, she lived on in Paris, participating in its literary life although, despite the urgings of friends, she did not reopen Shakespeare & Company. In 1956, she published a memoir of inter-war literary Paris, *Shakespeare & Company*. She died in Paris in 1962, aged 75.

Gisèle Freund

Freund returned to France at the end of World War II, after which she resumed her photographic career in Europe, although she continued to travel widely in Latin America. In 1950, Freund, working for *Life* magazine, photographed Eva Perón, wife of the then president of Argentina. The photographs, which showed Perón's vast collection of clothes, shoes and jewellery, caused an international controversy. Later, Freund was blacklisted in the United States for several years. In 1974, she published *Photography and Society,* her own study of the medium in which she had worked for so long. She retired from photography in 1980, saying she planned to spend the rest of her time reading. She died in Paris in March 2000, aged ninety-one.

The *Novus Angelus* by Paul Klee, which was owned by Walter Benjamin for many years, is now housed in the Israel Museum in Jerusalem. The quotation about this art work which appears on page 102 is taken from Benjamin's essay 'Theses on the History of Philosophy.'

The lines of poetry quoted on page 40 by Adrienne Monnier and Léon-Paul Fargue are taken from Fargue's poem, 'Romance'.

The lines quoted on page 119 are taken from Irmgard's Keun's *After Midnight*, first published in the Netherlands in 1937. Gisèle Freund was wrong in assuming that Keun had committed suicide. Keun faked her own death in order to remain underground in Germany during World War II. She died in Cologne in 1982.